JED COPE

The Legacy

They F you up your Mum and Dad...

1

The dirt in her hand was mostly clay. She had not attended to her actions and now, as she sought to separate it before dropping it into the hole in the ground, it failed to cooperate, instead it spread out into her hand refusing to bend to her will.

This simple act had gone awry and she felt that familiar feeling of anger rise up within her.

She let go of the clod of clay anyway, watching it drop onto the wooden lid of the coffin with a dull thud. The sound was impossibly loud and it was all wrong, it rang through her and she shuddered as though she'd been electrocuted. That shudder was not all the sound's doing though, her rage, the rage that was always close by, was now thrumming through her body.

She stared down into that hole for a long time. Doing just as her father had taught her. To look down so she would not be noticed by the harsh world and the cruel people who populated it.

The rage remained. It had nowhere else to go.

Now her father was dead, and she was totally alone. She would have been completely alone at this graveside had her mother, stepfather and half-brother not come along. She had assumed that they were here to provide her with support, that they were there for her. But then she had seen her mother's tears for a man she had divorced twenty years ago. A man who had actively shunned her, refused to acknowledge her existence, and hated her with a frightening vehemence even until his dying day.

Her father would have hated having these people anywhere near him, he couldn't have bared to look towards them and he would have turned tail and gotten as far away as possible, or failing that, he would have found a way to hide.

Just like he was now.

That was how Carol felt about all of this. She could not accept the fact of her father's death, there was so much unfinished business, the foremost of which was that she had never managed to fix him, to take away his hurt and see him happy again. She had never given up hope though, it was the reason that she was here on this earth. She had always seen the goodness in him. She just needed to unlock the door it was imprisoned behind and everything would be OK.

Then they would both start living the lives they were meant to live.

Now, her father was doing what he had always resorted to. He was hiding away from the world and she could not reach him, depriving her of a simple moment that would make everything alright again and take it back to a time before the divorce, to a halcyon time that she could no longer remember but believed with all her heart had existed. She had to, for without that, he had nothing, and she would have nothing.

Four people stood at the side of the man's grave. The day was not cold, but it wore a grey shroud that caused a person's very soul to grow cold. The grey had held the promise of rain and now it delivered upon that promise with a grim determination.

"We should go," Timmy touched her arm, saw the way Carol looked at his hand and withdrew it as though he'd been stung.

She stood for a little while longer, knowing the other three were keen to leave, but not wanting to do things on anyone else's terms. She was constantly seeking something in this life of hers, and one of the things she thought she wanted was control.

The three remaining members of her family waited for her patiently in the rain. None of them were dressed for today's weather and although the rain was not heavy, it was concentrated and persistent enough to soak through the dark suits that they all wore.

Carol watched the clump of dirt as the rain began to erode it and she thought that was a little like life. Life wore you away until there was precious little of you left. She had seen what it had done to her father and how painful that had been, even when Carol shared that same pain and anger, it had been too much for her father.

The large pile of earth next to her father's grave lay unnoticed and unremarked. Later, when the grave diggers came to fill the grave, there would be more than enough earth to fill the ground despite the rain's best efforts.

Eventually, Carol turned, barely looking up she walked past the waiting trio she got into the single funeral car. Her eyes remained downcast as what she considered to be her *other family* clambered into the back of the car with her, filling the space with unnecessary noise and a fug of damp, perfume, after shave and body odour.

As the car pulled away and headed to the back room of the pub for what would laughingly be called the wake, her mother tried to engage with her. She winced as her mother squeezed her leg as though she were still a child. The physical contact was alien to her and made her feel deeply uncomfortable. Her mother had never quite got it right. Touching her and trying to hug her when she was angry and completely unreceptive to that sort of demonstrative love, but failing to be there for her when she was very much needed. A cycle of abandonment and too-little-too-late, her mother had never really got her and didn't know her at all.

Her mother may not quite have been the cruel and callous harridan that her father and grandmother had portrayed her as from the very outset of the break up, but Carol had always found fault and weakness there. Fundamentally, her father was right about her mother, she was not to be trusted. Only he could be trusted, and he instilled this in Carol throughout her life, never letting up on this lesson, even beyond childhood.

4

Those tears of her mother's were real enough though and Carol would come back to those tears again, but not now. Now she was hurt and whenever things did not go away, in the face of any challenge, there was only anger. Carol was not a shouter, nor a screamer and she certainly did not throw things across the room, or kick or punch. All of those things were beneath her. So much was beneath her. She was her father's daughter and they were better than that.

And now her father had done the one thing that she had feared above all else.

Her father had left her and the anger she felt now was, she knew, only a precursor to a rage the likes of which she had never experienced before. Enduring and tolerating the next hour or so would be a trial. She could get through it though. Life was a trial and she was good at closing down all but her most essential of systems so it didn't much affect her. Carol had learnt how to hide in plain sight. She had coping mechanisms and ways of being that allowed her to navigate her way through the perils of social situations and out through the other side, back to the solitude of her own space. There she was most comfortable, away from the maddening crowds. Insulated from a species that on the face of it, she was a part of, but so very obviously was not. She was different and she was better. Just like her Dad. Only now, their population had been halved and she was a species on the verge of extinction.

The wake panned out exactly how she had envisaged. She had paid for the obligatory buffet and it did not disappoint. The food was mostly beige and filling. She spent the majority of her time grazing, a few items on her plate at any one time.

Thankfully the back room of the pub was intended for much larger groups and this gave her plenty of room. She did however have to field each of the three attendees of her father's funeral and their persistence grated upon her.

Timmy had asked her how she was. A ridiculous question in the circumstances and she had turned the question back on him swiftly.

"How do you think I am?"

She said this abruptly and with a callous intonation intended to wound. Timmy had however gotten used to this way of hers and took it in his stride, this was just how Carol was and she didn't mean anything by it. The thing was, she did mean something by it and her hackles went up and her levels of annoyance grew as Timmy feigned his ignorance and pretended that Carol was something that she most certainly was not.

"Don't tell Dad, but I've got a car that he would die for," Timmy grinned the very same grin he had always grinned. It made his eyes sparkle and lit up his face.

Carol hated him for that grin, not the misjudged words. As her father had always said, anyone who was as happy as Timmy was obviously missing the point of the world and somewhere a village was missing it's prize winning idiot.

"What car have you bought this time?" she sighed as she asked,

6

knowing he was going to tell her about the car, come what may.

He fumbled around in his inside suit pockets and then in his trouser pockets until he found his phone, swiping the screen and frowning as he concentrated on finding whatever it was he wanted to show her.

"Porsche 356!" he exclaimed as he showed her a photo of a gorgeous looking classically shaped car.

"It looks like a Beetle," Carol stated.

Disappointingly, this did not steal his thunder, "yeah, it does doesn't it!" he beamed.

Timmy had this with his Dad. This shared appreciation of cars, and motorbikes for that matter. Somehow Timmy had been steered away from riding motorbikes despite his father's love for them. Bob still rode motorbikes and called it part of his strategy to grow old disgracefully. He probably thought that this was a funny and endearing thing to say. It wasn't. Carol had hoped that this failure of Timmy's to embrace motorbikes would drive a wedge between the terrible twosome, but somehow they managed only to focus on the good bits and completely ignore the crap that didn't work between them. Her father had said that that was how it worked with fools and the criminally stupid.

Her father had also told her that there were a lot of very stupid people out there in the world. They were best avoided at all costs.

Her mother had walked over from the buffet and joined them, seeing Timmy making in-roads and making her own move on her daughter.

"What's all this then?" she asked them both.

Timmy showed her the photo on his phone.

"Is that yours?" her mother cooed this, it was painful for Carol to behold.

Her mother was a different person with Timmy, and Carol had never been comfortable with this person. Why couldn't she have made this sort of effort with her? It were as though she had embarked on a proper version of motherhood the second time around in order to spite her daughter. That nature had provided her with a happy-go-lucky son who skipped through the world without a care in the world was a travesty of natural justice. Carol would observe her half-brother from time to time and see nothing in him that she shared. He was supposed to be made from half of the raw materials that she had been made from and yet she saw none of that. She had frequently fantasised that there was a story here for her to uncover, that her life as she knew it was based on a lie. The single lie that had spawned so many others was that Emily was not her mother. Oh, they may have appeared to have some physical similarities, but so too did a great many people. There were only so many combinations of features and so Carol's passing resemblance to Emily was an irrelevance.

As with so many things in life, Carol had touched upon a truth of

8

sorts with her musings, and yet she were a million miles away from the real truth of the matter.

Emily smiled at Timmy, "you should show your dad that, he'll be really pleased for you."

"And green with envy!" Timmy grinned that idiot grin of his again as he literally skipped over to Bob. He really was behaving like the annoying little brother she had had to put up with whenever she had to stay at their house, which was damn near half of her life all the way up until she was fourteen.

She remembered the day she had told her mother that she was going to spend more time with her father. For some reason, Emily had been shocked and upset. Carol had expected her to be angry. After all, Carol was taking charge, she was taking control of the situation and Emily would not like that. Her father had warned her that this might happen, but instead Emily had whined and asked her why? As though it wasn't obvious. Why was her mother in such denial at her daughter's unhappiness whenever she had been forced to be in that house of hers?

"Because I want to," Carol had stated.

And that was that. Her mother may have spoken and tried to reason with her, but nothing and no one was going to change her mind.

"Look, I'll see you every other weekend, like most families do," Carol had cut in over the top of Emily as Emily had hurriedly scrolled through the internet on her phone and tried to tell her that she couldn't make a decision like this until she was sixteen, and that she was her mother and she loved her and blah, blah, blahdee, blah.

Emily and the idiotic twosome still had her visit every other weekend and that was more than enough as far as Carol and her father were concerned. She had even kept those visits up right until her sixteenth birthday. Then she had attained a level of blissful freedom that should have liberated her, but somehow failed to deliver.

"How are you, love?"

Now that Timmy had left them, her mother was in full sympathy mode. Carol knew this was an act, she'd left her Dad and she had behaved abysmally in the process breaking not only his heart, but him as a person. Abandoning them both and barely taking a pause before she moved on, meeting Bob several years later and even going on to marry the man. A person capable of that sort of thing wasn't genuine, could not experience true feelings, and they certainly could not be trusted.

"I'm fine," stated Carol.

"Oh love! Don't be like that! We're here for you, OK?"

Emily touched her arm in the exact same place that Timmy had. Apparently that was what you did to convey something like assurance and sympathy. They must have read the exact same self-help book on sympathetic touching. Again, she looked at the offending hand until it fell away.

1

Now Bob had joined the fray, at least this meant she could get the final interaction of the day over and after that she could leave and be on her own.

"How you holding up, Carol?" he asked.

Like he cared. He was the reason that her father never recovered from the break up. The bloody cuckoo in the nest who took over and prevented anything good ever happening again.

"Fine," stated Carol.

"Good," smiled Bob, "where are you staying?"

Carol gave Bob a dark look. It was the first time she had looked any of the three in the eye. The atmosphere in the room changed palpably and Carol thought she heard her mother draw in a sharp intake of breath at this development, a re-enactment of the bad old days in their house when Bob would challenge her for some minor indiscretion or offence and then embark on a failed attempt at making her more like him, spouting something about her behaving as he did so.

For his part, Bob did not react and annoyingly he stood there expectantly. Carol decided to put him out of his misery.

"At Dad's house," she told him.

"Oh, right..." Bob looked a little surprised.

Carol shook her head disdainfully, "it's mine now, so I'm going to live there," she announced loudly enough for all three of them to hear.

"That's good," said Emily, "it'll be lovely to have you back home."

"Yes," agreed Carol, meaning something completely different to her mother.

2

They say that losing a parent is transformative. That a person moves a step closer to death without the safe umbrella a parent provides, and with that pressing knowledge of their mortality a person sees the world in a very different way.

Carol's grief for her father did not cocoon her in a chrysalis state, readying her for the next stage of her life. She was unable or perhaps unwilling to separate her grief from the all too familiar anger she carried around with her always.

She did have anger towards her father and that was something that she explored and as she explored it, the first cracks in her fragile life appeared. Whether she would soldier on with those cracks as they were, was a mystery. It was certainly possible to live with cracks such as the ones that had developed in Carol's life, this had been played out many times before and would be played out again and again. People followed patterns and there were only a few real choices open to them through their lives. Very few people actively made those choices. Mostly life just happened despite the people who had been gifted it's fleeting miracle.

* * *

Carol was the sole heir to her father's estate. The estate comprised of a few items of furniture, a sizeable overdraft and the small terrace house that he had bought when he himself had inherited his mother's estate, also a small terrace house by the coast. He'd sold that and bought locally. He made a point of telling Carol that he would have kept his mother's coastal house and moved there had it not been for her. And then he conveyed to Carol the only future plan he ever seemed to have. When she was eighteen he would sell up and move back down to the coast. He didn't specifically say anything about blaming her for the existence he had to eke out here in the meantime, but he didn't have to. She knew well enough. She was the only reason he remained here.

That her father had not carried out this one step future plan of his did not surprise Carol one bit. Selling his house would have been tortuous for him. The very thought of dealing with people, relying upon them and being beholden to them on any basis was anathema to her father. So selling up, engaging an estate agent, having people invade the privacy of his personal space. Having to travel to the coast and search for a new house and make a fresh start.

It wasn't worth it.

Carol never once considered the practicalities of the plan itself. The selling fees would be considerable and properties on the coast were more expensive than they were here, especially in this part of town. Put simply, her father had never been able to afford to move back to the coast and he would have known this when he voiced his plan. That he had taken no steps to address this shortfall in funds meant that his plan was doomed to failure from the very start.

However, her father's failure to enact his plan presented Carol with the opportunity to return to a familiar space and pick up where she had left off. Moving out from her father's house had been a mistake of sorts. She had felt compelled to do so because, as she reached that landmark age of eighteen her father seemed to expand into the house that they shared, filling it with his latent anger and making it more and more difficult for Carol to be there.

He never said a word, he never had to, but over a protracted period, he edged her closer and closer to the door. Three years it took, a slow passive aggressive dance conducted in absolute silence. The fascinating thing was that they stopped arguing. There had always been low level arguments and short sharp bouts of bickering, but that was suffocated during the war that her father waged. The silence was the worst of it, that and Carol's belligerence. Her ability to dig in and stubbornly refuse to do anything let alone move was a wonderous thing, but then she had been taught by the best.

Turning the key in the door and entering the property that had been her only sanctuary from the world was a complete disappointment. Carol had turned the key in this lock and opened this door thousands of times, but this time it was different. It was all different. The feel of the key in her hand, the resistance of the lock and the door as she pushed it inwards. Carol had not expected her father to be there because he had never been there. Every time she had returned from a stay at her mother's house he had absented himself from the downstairs and either taken himself to the garden, or to his room. He did not want to risk an encounter with her mother. He could not bear the thought of seeing her and he told Carol a great many times that he did not believe in the existence of Emily, Bob, Timmy, their house nor the village they lived in. They were dead to him and so thoroughly dead that he had expunged their existence from his mind.

This was, he explained, a form of cleansing and it made him feel a whole lot better to have those people eliminated entirely from his life.

Carol had grown uncomfortable about this over the years. It had taken her a very long time to actually think about it properly, but when she did, she wondered how her life worked as far as her father was concerned. Did she wink out of existence when she was not with her father? Was this what everyone did in order to deal with their lives? She didn't think so, because she never stopped thinking about her Dad.

When she confronted him, it was a simple confrontation. She wanted her father to acknowledge her existence so they could talk. This was a reasonable request and driven by an honourable reason and her father had acceded to it with very little fuss.

2

Carol had been elated when at first he asked her how she had been and even asked about the dog, Bottie. Timmy had named the dog, much to the chagrin of Emily and the annoyance of Carol. The naming was slightly accidental, and Bottie displaced any attempt at an alternate name. The thing was that the dog responded to it from the off and worse still, it suited the silly dog. The worst of it was when the dog farted, Timmy would lapse into fits of the giggles whenever anyone would remonstrate with the flatulent dog. Exclaiming Bottie! Directly after a dog fart was comedy gold as far as Timmy was concerned.

It did not take Carol long to realise that although her father was making the effort to ask her about her time in limbo-land, that it was only ever lip service. He automatically trotted out the same questions and as she surreptitiously observed him as she answered, she could see that he did not care for her answers and only ever listened if he was in a particularly dark mood and was looking for ammunition. Material that he could tear up and remake as a weapon that perpetuated his hostility towards that specific part of this terrible world.

Eventually she followed suit and they lapsed into a short mean-ingless exchange and her father won not only that day, but all of the days. He had made his point. He was not interested and unless Carol came up with something he was interested in, there remained no point.

Carol loved her father with a vengeance. He was all she had in the world. So this was OK. It was OK that he wasn't interested in her because he wasn't interested in *people* and she had to agree with that sentiment.

Didn't she?

Today, as she entered the house, it was different because it was empty, and it was empty because her father was not here. Her father was dead and somehow this house was emptier than it would have been if her father had never been here in the first place, than if he had never existed. Somehow, he had managed to create an absence within the confines of the house. A polar opposite of the way he had fought and fought and made a concerted effort to fill it with a dark, brooding and threatening anger that had eventually driven her out. Now, in death, he had succeeded in creating a chasm that was just as frightening to her.

This emptiness was his parting gift.

His Legacy.

3

The day after her father's funeral, Carol walked into town and found herself a job.

She walked because she had never bothered to learn to drive. She could have, but she chose not to. That this created a bone of contention for Bob, helped secure her decision. Her father had walked and they were in agreement that roads were a gathering place for complete idiots and those idiots made it too dangerous for them to even consider driving.

They also shared the same view on their own abilities. They were a cut above the rest and if they were to deign to do a thing, they would not only do it well, they would do it better than everyone else. That this would not be appreciated by the cattle out there in this imperfect world was reason enough for them not to bother. What was the point? What thanks would they get for it? It was enough that they knew that they were better than everyone else. Showing that they were better would be dangerous. People didn't like that sort of thing. They couldn't deal with it.

The job she secured was behind the bar of one of the pubs in town. It did not escape Carol that her father had also worked behind this self-same bar. Of course he did, it was a short walk from the house and an easy way to earn sufficient money to pay the bills, so it ticked all the necessary boxes.

The bar was a funny old place. On the face of it, pubs were places where people socialised, and that was exactly what they did. From the safety of the other side of the bar though, Carol could observe these people and not get involved in their small lives and petty conversations. The bar itself placed a physical distance between her and this gathering place for social interaction. It was a fish tank and all Carol had to do was feed the fish and watch them dance around.

To say that it suited her, hiding there in plain sight, was an understatement. She derived a pleasure of sorts from her time behind the bar. She was always going to be good at what she did and she kept a good bar. She served the customers quickly, efficiently and in the order that they presented themselves.

She was professional and part of that professional persona was an aloofness that worked for the clientele of the pub. Occasionally she had to deal with bar flies, but mostly any transgressions were self-policing, other regulars stepping in to bring the miscreant back from the brink. They thought she did not notice them checking her out. This did not bother her at all and because she showed no reaction to appraising eyes she quickly became wallpaper.

Once she was referred to affectionately as 'one of their own'.

The smile she greeted this news with was unsteady and forced, and the moment passed swiftly for everyone else. For her it was a near fatal blow and that night she searched for alternative employment.

She lay staring at the ceiling of her childhood bedroom and she barely noticed her tears of rage. Being accepted and brought into the fold was so unfair. What had she done to deserve that? What had she done wrong? It seemed that the apparent protection of the bar was illusory and somehow those people had breached her defences and got in. She had been caught napping and she was mortified.

Carol didn't sleep well that night, but the next day she resolved to keep going. She needed the money and she wanted to hold down the same, steady job for as long as possible. Besides, she would do things on her terms and she needed to address this misconception that she was like those people, if she didn't then who was to say that it wouldn't happen in the next pub that she worked in?

A different approach was needed. She had obviously been too friendly.

* * *

The next morning, she was staring into space as she slowly ate her slice of toast. This for her, was a form of meditative state. She could shut off and block out the outside world very effectively. She barely registered the toast as she processed it.

She did register the doorbell however.

Who the hell could that be?

She thought for a moment, she had no deliveries due. So that ruled out the only valid reason for someone to ring her doorbell. She looked down at the remaining toast as though it may be able to provide a solution to this conundrum. The doorbell rang again. The time elapsed between the two doorbell rings was significant, but Carol did not allow for this and deemed it rude and impatient, and so it was with this in the forefront of her mind that she answered the door.

The door swung open with a swish of aggressive energy.

"What do you want?" hissed Carol, there was a silent *hell* in her sentence and almost everyone would have spotted that and reacted to it.

Almost everyone.

"Hello Carol! We thought we'd pop over to say hi!" her Mum was smiling as she said this.

Carol's brow creased. We? Framed in the doorway was her mother. Had she begun to use the Royal We? Was she turning into Granny? This would not surprise Carol one bit, her mother looked more and more like Granny every time she saw her. Carol thought that her mother descending into the weird and wonderful world of her Granny may be a blessing for everyone concerned.

"Are you going to let us in then?" asked her mother.

Carol thought about this and did not move or respond, so her Mum took the initiative and stepped over the threshold. As Carol recoiled from her approaching mother, she saw Bob enter the frame of the doorway and then step inside the house. This caused her a physical jolt and she felt her arms raising involuntarily. With a force of will she restrained their movement and so too did she still the word forming at her lips.

No.

Her Dad.

Her Dad would have been angry. He would have been more than angry. Few people ever, ever came into their house and any that did came in under sufferance. This applied even to his long-time girlfriend, Hilary. Her father and Hilary quickly came to an understanding and an arrangement that saw them keeping to their own houses and meeting up in short bursts to have some time together. This had worked for her Dad. Carol saw that it did not seem to work for Hilary and she sometimes wondered why someone would put up with something if it did not work for them. But put up with it she did, for over a decade she did, so somehow it must have suited Hilary too.

Only now did Carol wonder why Hilary hadn't been at her Dad's funeral. Yes, they hadn't been seeing each other for a few years now, but over ten years together was a big part of someone's life. That thought passed through Carol's mind and it and any other related thoughts were gone. Carol had more pressing matters to attend to. She never thought of Hilary again.

Retreating to the kitchen as the combined forces of her mother and step dad invaded her Dad's house, she regrouped at the kettle. She was filling it and preparing three mugs of tea before she realised what she was doing. This ridiculously stupid act was guaranteeing at least another ten minutes of them being here in this space. With her.

"Don't I get one?" said another, familiar voice.

Timmy had come in behind his parents and spotted the three mugs on the kitchen side. Carol didn't bother responding and her only acknowledgement of Timmy was to retrieve a further mug from the cupboard and drop a tea bag into it. This was looking like a family intervention and her hackles, which were always in an alert state, were firmly up.

"You know," said Bob, in an attempt to fill the awkward silence, "this is the first time I've been inside this house in all these years."

"I've never been in the kitchen," said her Mum.

And Carol remembered the time she had brought her Mum into the house to show her a flower she had found on a walk with her Dad, and pressed between the pages of a book. It was the only time her Mum had come into the house, her Dad made

24

sure that Carol was very clear on the rules after that. As though to underline the importance of keeping his sanctuary free of anyone, but in particular her mother, that flower was taken away by the treasure fairy soon afterwards. The treasure fairy took things that did not belong and when Carol spotted the absence of some of her treasures she made a concerted effort to leave the things she found when she was at her Mum's, in her bedroom there. Once she understood the rules, the treasure fairly seldom visited again.

"Neither have I," said Timmy.

Timmy had been up to her room a few times and her Dad seemed to make an exception to this whilst Timmy was *of an age.* Carol wasn't sure when this age ended, but it seemed to be around the time that Timmy grew as tall as her Dad. Maybe it was as his voice broke. All Carol knew was that one day Timmy was almost welcome in her Dad's house, and the next he most certainly wasn't. She knew that the withdrawal of the welcome was irrevocable as far as her father was concerned.

Well this is awkward, she thought to herself as she handed out the steaming mugs of tea to the other half of her family whilst they sat in the entirely *wrong place.*

That they did not belong here was obvious. She could not, for the life of her, understand how they could sit here like it was the most natural thing in the world to do when it was so incredibly unnatural. Parts of her were threatening to cramp up with the anxiety of it all.

"So," said Carol, grabbing this particular bull by the horns, "why are you here?"

Her mother did not miss a beat. Carol's delivery had been harsh and intended to provoke but she rode over that to more certain ground, "well, we haven't seen you in over a month. Not since the... you know."

"Dad's funeral," Carol supplied the circumstances of the last time they had met, "I've texted you since."

"That's not the same though is it? We thought we'd give you some time to settle in, but then Bob pointed out how long it had been. Doesn't time fly!?"

"It does when you're our age!" Bob grinned as though this were a good thing.

Dad would have been so annoyed at having been outlived by Bob, thought Carol. Where this thought had come from she did not know. She thought it may be the spirit of her Dad, speaking to her as he rolled in his coffin, aggrieved at the desecration being committed in his house. Just because he was dead, well there was no excuse for breaking his most sacred of rules.

The kitchen descended into silence again. Silence was good as far as Carol was concerned, she had all the soundtrack she needed with the myriads of thoughts in her head. The spoken word was very much overrated.

"How are you settling in?" asked her Mum, invading the silence and doing it with an expectation that Carol would aid and abet her in this invasion.

"Well enough," she sipped at her tea. Disappointed that it was too hot to take swigs from and hasten the moment of her family's departure.

"That's good!" her Mum smiled as though by smiling she could make it true that it was good.

"Have you found a job?" it was Timmy that asked this. Of course it was Timmy. With his impressively successful car business. He bought and sold classic and prestige cars and apparently, his enthusiasm and affection for those cars was infectious. Carol was of course immune to this passion of his. She didn't see the point to it. He made a point of saying he was happy and that was what success was about for him, that he did something that *switched him on.* If he needed switching on then he was obviously not human. That would explain a lot.

"Yes," said Carol.

Timmy looked askance. He had offered Carol a job after the funeral. Tried calling her, but she didn't pick her phone up for calls. Ever. That was what voicemail was for. It allowed calls to be vetted and circumvented any intrusion. Carol regained control in this way. It was always her decision as to whether she replied and when it was that she would reply. In this case, she did not reply. She also failed to respond to her half-brother's texts on the matter of potential employment in his firm. His texts referenced an email he had sent which apparently outlined some thoughts on how they could form a Dream Team.

In his dreams!

As if she was going to accept. Carol could see Timmy's offer for exactly what it was. If she accepted then she would forever be tarnished by it, she would have officially accepted his view of the world and in his view Carol was second best. He was the golden boy and this would be proof positive of that. He'd employed Carol, what a good boy he was!

Carol sighed, they wouldn't let up until they knew what she was doing to pay the bills, "I'm working at the Falcon. For now." She added those last two words because although she had paused her immediate desire to leave and find another pub with a more effective bar to work behind, she was not precluding this course of action. She was the mistress of her destiny after all.

"Bring in some cash while you find your feet?" asked her Mum.

"Something like that," said Carol, doing her best to sound like she agreed whilst doing nothing of the sort.

"What kind of work are you looking for?" it was Bob who asked, but the words could have been Timmy's. Chip off the old block and all that. She could feel Timmy's expectant eyes, and her mother's too.

"I'm not," said Carol bluntly, and Carol's blunt was breezeblock blunt.

There was a short pause, barely the length of a breath, but it was pregnant with all sorts of bastard babies. Carol could feel them all judging her. They all knew better and they wanted to foist upon her a way of being that could never suit her. Them with their saccharine sweet lives. They were dog people and if Carol had the time and inclination for a pet, well, she'd be a cat person. It was obvious really.

Carol regularly wondered why everyone else chose to ignore the obvious. She refused to believe that they could not see these things, so the only conclusion was that they were ignorant. This made sense to her as time and again, she saw displays of wilful ignorance. If she had been more honest with herself, she got very frustrated when people defied her control. She wanted them to do something, and yet they went and did something else. Life worked so much better for other people, why was she so bloody unlucky?

Take now for instance, her family making camp in her Dad's kitchen and quizzing her over her life choices. She knew what was coming and it wasn't going to be pretty.

Her mother drew in a breath and Carol watched Bob pull back, he had been about to speak, but instead deferred to his wife, "I fully understand you taking a time out, but have you thought about what it is you're going to do next?"

"Do next?" Carol felt defensive and belligerent, who were these people to come here and challenge her about her life?

"Carol, you have a degree..." Bob left the sentence hanging, left it to speak for itself. People with degrees didn't settle for bar work.

"Only because you made me get a degree!" Carol protested.

Bob's face crumpled, he had not expected this.

Good, thought Carol, he needed to know that it was his fault. His fault that she had left the area for three years and broken her Dad's heart. She had gone despite her Dad. Had known that he didn't want her to go, even though it left him free to enact his plan to sell up and move to the coast. That was why Carol had gone. They had an agreement and this was what she was supposed to do. Only her Dad stayed put and turned it into a betrayal. Carol had abandoned him. It was as though this were the real plan and she was following a script. Her departure was preordained. Everyone left her Dad, so why would she be any different?

Things were never the same after that and Carol blamed Bob. Bob had orchestrated Carol's departure and driven a wedge between her and her Dad. The wedge did not plunge between them instantaneously, although the wealth of the damage was done on the day she left for university. That she stuck it out and got a degree made it worse, because it was during this period that Carol surpassed her Dad's achievements. She got a degree and that somehow diminished her. She had broken rules and no longer followed the creed. Her Dad's creed: being fully capable of doing something, but making a point of not doing it. Carol would always be second rate for having gone out and got a degree, as though she had something to prove. That was weak.

If her Dad had not known better, she would start following her dreams and be enthusiastic about what she did with her days. Her Dad had a way of saying *enthusiastic* in a way that made it sound like the worst kind of swear word. Her Dad had a way of saying a lot of things in a way that weaponised them.

Carol missed her Dad right now. She missed him more than she ever had. The presence of these people brought it home to her that he was not here and he never would be. Once again, these people stood in the way of her Dad, and her resentment was reaching boiling point.

Bob sighed, "why do you have to fight us? We only want you to be OK. That's all we've ever wanted."

"Well I am," Carol fired the words out like bullets.

"I just thought..." Bob began.

"What? That now my Dad's dead I'll do what you want?" Carol stared at Bob like he was dirt.

This was not new to Bob, but it didn't stop it landing and it hurt just as surely as it would if she'd cut him.

"Carol, please..." her mother reached out a hand to touch Carol's, but Carol recoiled from the suggestion of physical contact. She didn't need it, "I know this is a difficult time, we came here to help. We're here if you need us, OK?"

Carol looked at her mother, but there was no acknowledgement in that look. She looked down at her mug and was pleased to see that it was nearly empty. She made a point of drinking the last of the contents, getting up and putting it in the sink. She then took all of the remaining three mugs from her visitors. That the mugs were not empty did not phase Carol, even if it was contrary to the mores and norms in the bar. Taking a patrons half consumed pint could lead to dire consequences. This was different though.

This was family.

She stood, arms folded, awaiting their departure.

Eventually, they got the message. Their withdrawal was awkward and sloppy, but at last they went.

"Bye," she said to their backs as they left the house and she shut the door.

As she returned to the kitchen to wash the mugs and remove any evidence of their presence in her Dad's house her phone bleeped a notification.

It was a text from her half-brother Timmy:

Great to see you, sis. Let's talk about opportunities in the family firm soon! Let me know when you're free for a drink? T

Carol closed the app and turned off her phone and got to the more important business of cleansing the mugs. Timmy was likely telling his Dad and her Mum all about his charity efforts

3

and they were doubtless lapping it up and telling him how wonderful he was. Well they could all bugger off as far as she was concerned. She fumed as she scrubbed the mugs clean.

4

There was no escaping it, people were complete and utter idiots.

Carol had decided to give The Falcon and it's patrons another chance. She had granted them a stay of execution and she'd gone in for her next shift safe in the knowledge that this was her gainful employment for the foreseeable future.

And it were as though they *knew!*

They seemed to know that she was not on form having been rattled by her family's earlier intrusion and unsuccessful intervention. They also seemed to know that they were on probation and from the outset they were overly nice to her. However much she rebuffed their attempts at conversation and the clumsy olive branches, they just didn't get it.

The manager was the final straw.

She had taken Carol to one side at the end of her shift.

"Just wanted a word," she began.

Carol had nodded and awaited the word.

"You're doing really well here and I... well, I just wanted to thank you for your work and well, I've spoken with head office about you and they agree with me that your talents should be recognised, so I... we'd like to offer you a promotion and a place on the management trainee program."

There was an awful silence, during which Carol's eyes bored into her manager in a way that intended for the manager to be minus her head, if those eyes had anything to say about it that was.

Her manager was slow on the uptake. Of course she was, or else she would not have pulled this stunt. Carol could see it now. Bob, thwarted earlier that day by Carol as he attempted a direct frontal assault to get his own way, had then hot footed it here and pulled strings, persuading this woman to do his dirty work for him. Well she was blowed if she was going to be made to conform to anyone else's view of how she should live her life!

"What is it?" her manager sounded aghast, almost as though she were surprised by Carol's reaction.

"Why have you done this?!" Carol said this as though the manager had clubbed a kitten to death in front of her.

"Well..." the manager looked uncomfortable and quite rightly so, "...you're good at what you do. And you've got a degree..."

"How do you know that!?" barked Carol.

"It was on your CV," explained the manager.

"Look, I came here to work in the bar. It's that simple. Now I discover that you're stalking me. Reading my CV for no good reason. That's a breach of my data rights, right there. Not content with that, you've gone behind my back and spoken about me to other people."

Carol let those words sink in.

"It wasn't like that," the manager wheedled.

"It's exactly like that. You've breeched my trust and I quit."

"You what?" this exchange had not gone at all like the manager had expected and she was floundering in unchartered waters. She watched as Carol turned tail and flounced out of The Falcon, never to darken its doors again.

* * *

Bar work wasn't difficult to find.

Keeping it was more difficult.

People was what made it difficult. Carol remembered one of her Dad's golden rules: look down. Looking down kept you out of

36

harm's way. Looking down meant that you didn't get noticed and it gave you a rest from all the unnecessariness of the world.

Carol remembered her Dad waxing lyrical about the benefits of looking down on numerous occasions when they went for their walks. Those walks were like a safari for Carol, only they were braver than most and had dispensed with the jeep, instead they walked amongst the wild animals and got really close to them without ever being seen.

The looking down strategy at the new bar seemed to work for a while and she was left well alone. She was pleased to note the absence of comments claiming her as one of the customers' own. That didn't happen, but complaints did.

Carol was missing people when they came to the bar. She ignored people. And the manager of her latest pub job even had the temerity to say that she made people feel awkward. He even went a step further than that...

"Look, you're on the spectrum, I get it. My cousin is a bit special and he's definitely not front of house material. I think we're going to have to let you go. Maybe look for something more suited to your condition, you know?"

"I could go to HR about this," said Carol coldly.

"Not really you couldn't," said the manager.

"Why not?"

"Because HR is the landlord," said the manager pointedly.

"And?"

"He's my Dad?" the manager smiled smugly which did not endear him at all to Carol.

"That's beside the point," Carol wouldn't let him off the hook that easily.

"Look," the manager leaned towards her, "I'm doing this for your own good. I could have just sacked you with no explanation, but I don't want you going through this again and again. You've been here two months, you have no employment rights, OK?"

"You can't say those things though," Carol said glaring at the man in front of her. He'd been unfair and she wanted him to know it.

He sighed nonchalantly and straightened, the exchange coming to an end as far as he was concerned, "say what things?"

"What things?!" cried Carol, "you just told me I'm on the spectrum and a *bit special!*"

"I tried to be open and fair. But I can see that that was a mistake and there's no helping you," the manager did that smug smile of his again, "as for those things you *say* that I said? I didn't. Not a word. I merely told you that you are surplus to requirements. Nothing else. Shit happens."

Carol wanted to say something further, but knew there was nothing much else to say, "fine!" she barked and with that she left The Cauldron, never to darken its door again.

* * *

Of course, Carol did not take the manager of The Cauldron's advice and her very next job was in a pub, as were the two jobs after that. It was only when she had run out of pubs that were in a reasonable distance of her house, either by walking or on a bus route, that she had, by necessity, to consider alternative employment. This she did by walking the local area and reconnoitring potential sources of gainful employment.

This was how, a week later, her mother discovered her behind the counter of the baker's, selling freshly baked bread and cakes and making sandwiches at lunchtime for the local office workers and passing trade. She had just finished making butties for three large men in high viz jackets and dusty boots with the leather worn from over their steel toe caps when her mother appeared at the counter.

"Hello you!" she beamed at her daughter.

Not an exemplar of excellent customer service, Carol responded with the blunt yet practical, "what do you want?"

Emily looked taken aback, not that Carol noticed this. Carol had become so adept at ignoring people and in particular her mother, that she was oblivious to the effect that she had on anyone. This ignorance meant that she hadn't learnt to modify or moderate her behaviour and the tone and timbre of her voice could itself be harsh and unfriendly. For some reason though, this tone of hers managed to convey some degree of authority and more by accident than management, it sometimes helped carry her through life regardless of her intent.

Flustered, and in being flustered, judged by her daughter to be an old fool, Emily looked around the glass fronted counter and panic bought several items.

"I'll have two of those, and those... I may as well have one of those too," she looked up at the shelves behind Carol and spotted a solitary and forlorn looking loaf in the shape of a swirl with black seeds on the top that looked far too much like mouse droppings to have been a good idea, "I'll have that loaf too, please."

Carol looked around, surprised that there were any loafs left, they were usually out of fresh bread by late morning.

"Will that be all?" asked Carol as she handed her mother the loaf.

Emily nodded, wanting the transaction to be over so she could perhaps have a civil conversation with her daughter. As Carol handed her mother her change, marvelling at how she had used cash instead of the card almost everyone else used, a voice piped up from behind the trays of bread, emanating from the bakery itself.

"You may as well head off now, Carol," said the disembodied voice, "lunchtime rush is over."

Carol tried not to cringe, but failed abysmally.

For her part, Emily was beaming at this moment of fortuitous happenstance, "let's grab a nice cuppa and have a mother and daughter chat!"

Carol actually scowled at her mother, and as she did, most of her years rolled from her and she was exposed as the churlish little child we perhaps all are underneath the brave adult exterior.

"Good!" Emily continued to beam, almost as though she saw something completely different to the reality that surely presented itself to her in that moment, and she did. She saw her child. Her daughter. Emily was from that sizeable school of parents who, however old and big their child became, always saw the small, defenceless acorn that had needed nurturing and protection and most of all unconditional love. For some, that part never left and if ever forgotten, it was not far away and would be summoned whenever needed.

Emily had doubted her ability to be a parent, had been daunted by it and doubted that she could ever be good enough. When she took the plunge, she did it with a good deal of forethought and hadn't ceased thinking about it since. To her it was the most difficult thing in the world and it brought great worry and sometimes pain. It was also the greatest privilege she could ever have imagined, right from the get go. She had carried a life within her and felt it grow day by day! She had loved being pregnant, her worries had really begun when she considered the chapters after that. Her child, out in the world. The thought of the risk and pain her child would be exposed to was too much to bear at times. And yet, she learnt that she could not live her child's life for her, she could not be there one hundred percent of the time, but she could do the next best thing and that was to be the best parent she possibly could to her child, so that she was there even when she wasn't there. That she had loved with all her heart and put in as much time, effort, energy and patience as she possibly could and in so doing also provided a good example, that should have been enough.

That should have been enough.

Carol looked at her mother and knew that the path of least resistance was to go along with her. Anything else would be awkward and despite her chosen inability to shun the mores and norms of the world and walk her own path, she generally tried to avoid conflict. Although it may have seemed otherwise to the uncaring world, conflict took its toll on Carol. Everything took its toll on Carol, Carol most of all.

And so, two people who looked so similar in some respects and yet were so different in others, left the bakery and walked across the road to a small, independent tea shop, Emily loved the fact that it was independent, but better still it had the balls to be a tea shop in a world of coffee shops. The two women may have been headed for the same destination, but the way they made their way over that short distance spoke volumes. There was a distance between the two of them and no semblance of togetherness as they traversed the close confines of a narrow pavement that tried its best to bring them together, but somehow could not.

5

As they took their seats at the Tea Shop, the usual patterns were observed and Carol drew her battle line. She took the seat opposite her mother and sat sullenly and tense. Unmoving, she did not even glance at the menu that was placed before her.

In contrast, her mother deployed the energy of hustle and bustle and enthused about a menu that she could have written herself. There were no surprises to be had on a menu of teas and other hot and cold beverages. The cakes were standard fare also. That though was missing the point. This was not any old mug of tea made in the comfort of her own kitchen. She had had thousands upon thousands of those and although she valued them, each and every one, for they were part of the comfort of her home, this pending tea was special because it was a tea taken out and it was a tea taken out with her daughter.

"What would you like, Carol?" Emily asked her daughter.

"Tea," said Carol, she still had not even glanced at the plastic coated menu.

"Good choice!" enthused her mother, "shall we treat ourselves to something naughty? Scones with jam and cream, perhaps?"

"Mum, I work in a bakery," said Carol in a dour tone.

Emily pulled up short, not quite following the logic. She looked askance of her daughter, found no help there, so instead joined the dots for herself, assuming Carol helped herself to the items in the bakery. She shrugged, "well, I'll have a blueberry muffin then, and you can have some if you'd like."

"I won't," said Carol.

Emily smiled in response and recalled the girl Carol had been. Carol had always been like the woman that sat opposite her now was, however much Emily, Bob and Timmy had tried. Yes, she'd had moments where she forgot herself and the child that she was and the person she could be and perhaps should have been now, shone through. It was the blueberry muffin that made Emily think of that now. Carol had loved blueberries and that had been enough for her mother. To see her face light up with pure, unalloyed joy at the sight of blueberries. Add the blue delights to a muffin and Carol went off the scale as she saw the way the juice of the blueberries seeped into the muffin itself, imbuing it with its distinctive colour and the promise of a tasty treat that would be second to none.

Emily had wanted more of that for her daughter. She could see that child, and wondered why she was trapped inside a harsh exterior, frightened to come out and experience the world. Emily had always wondered why Carol continually chose to retreat from being in the world, but deep down she knew, or at least suspected why.

It had been the divorce. Emily could have been brash and unthinking and left it at that, but even now the pain of her failures and the weight of the guilt she carried and the responsibility she had for causing not just her life, but the life of Jacob and their daughter Carol to implode, forced her to confront her part in the situation.

Emily had over egged her part in that particular situation and her guilt and the need it drove to make amends blinded her to the wider situation. She knew that damage was being done even before the divorce, that the way she and Jacob were behaving made a split inevitable and once the split occurred, there was no going back. Not for them. It was the aftermath that caused the real problems for Carol though. There was a half of Carol's life that was a black box to Emily and probably always would be. Emily knew that Jacob loved his daughter and had trusted that he would always do right by her. By the time she began to realise that maybe this expectation of hers was not being fulfilled as well as it might be, she came to a terrible realisation, that it was too late to do anything about it, Carol had a life to live and she would have to find her own way, making mistakes along the way like everyone did. Only, it very much felt like Carol was intent on not learning and that was the biggest mistake anyone could make.

The problem, one of the problems as there was not a singular problem, was how did Emily talk to Carol about any of this when she knew full well that her words fell against the shell that Carol had retreated into. This was not a case of words falling upon deaf ears. Emily could find no ears to speak the words to. This did not stop her trying though. It never had.

The tea arrived, in a pot. Alongside it was placed a large muffin with blueberries erupting from its top. Emily smiled at the muffin as though it were an old friend or the ghost thereof.

"How are you coping dear?" Emily cringed inwardly at the words. They were the words of her own mother. The words of an old woman. Emily supposed that she was indeed that woman, but this did not help her much in this instance.

This time, when Carol raised her eyebrows and pulled a grim face, Emily fully got it. As an opening line, it sucked and if she was being graded she'd expect the teacher to write *see me* and she would dread that meeting with the teacher.

Emily tried again, "I just thought that now... you know..."

Carol had her *in* and she wasn't going to waste it, "what? That now... you know... my Dad is dead?"

"I didn't mean it like that," said Emily sounded defeated.

"Well, how did you mean it then?" challenged Carol.

Emily poured the tea, half a cup, then a full cup and then back to the half cup. That way they both got a good strength tea, well that was her theory on pouring from the pot anyway. The tray had come with another pot of boiled water which she added to the pot, she did not see Carol scowl at this attempt at prolonging the agony of their interaction. Milk added she pushed Carol's tea towards her and took up her own to take a sip.

Now slightly more composed, she spoke again, "I suppose you're right. I might have meant it like that."

"What?!" Emily had surprised Carol with her candour.

"Your Dad wasn't an easy man to live with, was he?" explained Emily.

"You would say that," Carol almost growled these words.

Emily had started, so she persevered, "he could be very quiet, and when we parted company, he seemed to withdraw all the more. That's what I saw anyway and you never said anything, so I assumed that this was just how he was. But..."

"But what?" there remained a growl to Carol's words and her tea remained untouched, she was staring at her mother and trembling with an unconcealed angry energy. All attempts at its concealment completely forgotten.

Emily was so used to Carol's anger that she did not give it much heed. She'd lived with it constantly and nothing and no one could do anything about it because Carol owned it completely and would not let it go. Emily suspected she knew some of the cause of the anger, but this anger of Carol's was self-perpetuating and very, very clever. It used denial adeptly and it trumped all else.

"But you never said anything. I always wondered about that. Even when we asked you about you and how you were and gave you all the reassurance in the world, there was something between us. I always thought it was me and it took your Dad dying for me to see that I might have been wrong."

Her face crumpled and Carol watched as her Mum began to cry.

Embarrassed was what Carol thought she was as she witnessed this, but then, through her rage she felt this rising indignation.

"Don't you dare cry over my Dad!" now she was growling.

How dare this woman cry mock tears over a man she betrayed so badly she broke him. How dare this woman cry when she had not only betrayed her Dad, but also betrayed her and left her to pick up the pieces.

Emily dabbed her eyes with a tissue from her voluminous handbag, "I'm not crying for your Dad, I'm crying for you. And me. I failed you and I still don't know how I did. Only that somehow I did. I missed something that sat there between us all of the time you were growing up and it's there even now. I'd thought..." she sighed and the sigh hit a waiting sob that she had to swallow down to prevent further tears.

"That it was my Dad?" said Carol coldly.

"No. Not him," said Emily decisively, "but that with his passing there would be a change."

What Emily wanted to say was something about Carol emerging from under Jacob's shadow. That his death would release her from the hold he'd had upon her. But that hadn't happened and even beyond the grave, Carol was living the life that her father had pre-ordained for her. Emily supposed that this was what parents did and if that was the truth of it, then she had two questions. What had happened to her input as a parent, where had that gone? And once parents had done their worst, what could a child do to vary their path and break away from some of the harm that had been gifted to them?

Carol harrumphed.

Emily looked towards her daughter earnestly, thought about reaching her hand out to hold her little girl's, but the teapot, cups and muffin formed a practical barrier to that sign of affection and support.

"I just want you to be OK. That's what I have always wanted for you. That's what a mother wants for her child. That they can go out into the world and have choices and find fulfilment and perhaps a little success, whatever form success takes for them."

"What? Like dear little Timmy?" snarled Carol.

"Yes, exactly like Timmy," agreed her mother, not rising to the bait.

"Oh come on, mother! Timmy isn't a success! Dad always said he was the little blue eyed boy who never grew up! You still call him Timmy! What kind of a man is called Timmy!? He never grew up to be a Tim, did he!?"

Emily squared her shoulders and rounded on Carol, Timmy was her child as well and she did not take kindly to anyone speaking ill of any of her family, but especially not her children. That Carol had invoked her Dad in this and given some credence to Emily's suspicions stoked her fires even more. Jacob had been silent when it came to Emily and Emily's family. His silence had been a wall behind which he poured poison into their daughter's ear. She could see that now, and now she had heard Jacob's words from Carol's mouth.

Emily fought the urge to defend her second born, but she could not help herself, "and how do you define success?"

Carol had landed a potentially killing blow, and her mother had railed against this. She looked uncertain just for a moment and then her face creased into something approximating a snarl.

"Oh! That's it! Why don't you compare me with Golden Boy!"

Emily shook her head, trying not to show her disappointment. It was Carol that had set up the comparison and then pounced on her. She was tired of these traps and the arguments, even after the break that Carol seemed intent on continuing to enforce.

"I don't want to argue with you. Quite the opposite. I want to hold out an olive branch. Whatever I've done wrong. Whatever you think of me. Let's put that behind us and start again? We're both grown women now. Can't I at least be your friend?"

"No."

That was Carol's final word on the matter and the speed with which she left the scene of this crime was as callous as the crime she had just committed.

6

N o.

Carol stared up towards the ceiling, but it was not the ceiling that she was seeing. Her eyes were misted over with unseeing right now, instead with her mind she was visualising that *no* and what it had meant as she said it and what it meant for her now.

A single word that had made such an impact. A word that reached all the way back to a hazy time before her memories and reached out far into the future. There was a darkness to that word. A shroud.

Carol felt numb and confused.

Saying no to her mother and putting her in her rightful place should have felt good at the time, and the feeling she had expected to feel after that moment never came. There was no release. She did not feel lighter, instead she felt heavier.

This flew in the face of the received wisdom. Weren't you

supposed to feel better when you let something or someone go?

And yet here she was, laying in her bed and feeling angrier than she thought was possible. This anger was her mother's fault. She had caused this. She had tried to...

Her mother had said things that she shouldn't have.

Her mother was not to be trusted and yet again she'd caused Carol pain.

For the first time since her father's death and for the first time in a long, long time Carol cried genuine tears. In the confusion of her dark thoughts the tears sprouted and with them some respite from those thoughts of hers. Her constant companions, her thoughts were not her friends and they seldom left her be, now though there were only those tears and an overwhelming grief.

Carol cried herself asleep that night.

And she dreamt.

* * *

That she would dream was a foregone conclusion – her permanently, barely stocked cupboards and fridge were at a low point and all she had had available for dinner that night was a block of cheddar that had been left open and gone shiny and hard. She washed it down with some orange squash and turned in for the night with the intention of buying provisions tomorrow as long as a member of her rogue family did not attempt to hijack her day again.

At first she was not aware of her transportation through the curtains of consciousness to a sleeping state because she remained exactly where she was, laying in that bed of hers and staring up at a ceiling that at times had been her entire world.

When the door to her bedroom opened, she was not at all surprised, especially when she saw the figure of her Dad in the doorway. She had after all experienced this moment a million times before.

Her Dad stood at the doorway, frozen in time. He spoke not a word.

"Dad?" Carol spoke the word tentatively, trying to understand what was happening and why her Dad looked so grave.

Her spoken word did not break the spell.

Her Dad did not move and he remained framed in the doorway. Carol sat up thinking this would allow her to see more clearly and in seeing more clearly an explanation as to her father's strange behaviour would be forthcoming.

Still nothing happened other than Carol's concerted efforts to understand the picture that was being presented to her. Her father had been prone to bouts of silence, but this silence had a different quality to it. This was an ominous and weighty silence. The silence of the grave.

And that was when a wave of something like realisation swept over her. Her father was dead and buried in the ground, and yet here he was before her and in the flesh, for there was something very real about this experience, more real than real.

Carol sat there, shocked and willing her own body to move, if only to tremble a little with the terror that she now felt. Her father had come back from the grave to haunt her, but why?

As though awaiting this acknowledgement of hers, Jacob walked into her bedroom and to the foot of her bed as in life he had done so many times before.

"Dad," said Carol again.

The grey figure shook its head and in the eerie light of her bedroom, Carol could see that this was the pallor of her father's skin, he was stained grey with a darkness.

"What has happened to you, Dad?" Carol's voice sounded strange to her as she spoke, her voice was a former voice. The voice of her as a little girl.

Daddy's little girl.

"I happened to me," said her Dad sadly.

"What do you mean?" asked Carol, her voice now trembling, not with fear but with an icy cold that had seeped into the bedroom and into her bones, her teeth were threatening to chatter and she clenched them together so as not to have them interfere with her exchange with her Dad. An exchange she would have given anything to have, but now that she was gifted it, she was in turmoil. There was something dark about this figure. This was not the Dad she knew and loved.

"You are right," said the figure, "I am not the Dad that you knew in life."

Carol's brow knotted and she gasped at the surprise of the figure's *knowing,* she could not say anything further, frozen for the moment by the figure's words.

"You did not know me, my daughter. I didn't allow you to and for that alone I will pay."

"Pay? What do you mean you will pay?" Carol didn't like the way that sounded and she didn't like the forlorn sound of her father's voice. His demeanour spoke of a brokenness that went well beyond anything that she had seen in life. Something terrible had happened to her father.

"Yes, something terrible happened to me," agreed the figure, reading her thought yet again, "I happened to me again and again and again."

"What do you mean?!" cried Carol, wanting this to stop. Her father sounded so sorry for himself and so sad. She wanted this to stop right now!

"That," was all the figure said, raising a bony finger to point at Carol.

Carol looked at the spot on her chest that her father was pointing at.

In response the grey figure cackled with an awful laughter.

"What!? What is it?!" Carol cried as she was laughed at for a protracted while.

"You are so literal at times. That always made me laugh!" this sounded so like her Dad that Carol's chest nearly burst with the hurt of it.

"It really is you isn't it, Dad?"

"No. I am dead, daughter. This is what I am become. Only, I fear I have yet to see the full extent of it, but it is only what I deserve."

"I don't understand!?" wailed Carol in her confusion at her father's words.

"That is why I am here. So you may understand and avoid this fate of mine," groaned her father.

"Are you in pain? Does it hurt?" asked Carol at the sound of that groan.

"It always has," said her ghostly father in response.

"Why didn't you say anything?" gasped Carol.

"You knew well enough, child. You have always known."

"Known what?"

Her father sighed and something rattled within him as he did so, "they said this would be difficult."

"Who did? Who sent you, father?"

"I came of my own volition. I begged them. They told me it was pointless. That I could not make you change."

"Change? Change what? Why would I change?"

Her father ignored her questions, "they said that I made you this way and that you were exactly like me, so why did I not see there was no hope here..." he groaned a long and low groan, "oh! What have I done! Will this ever end!"

"Dad! What's happening? Are you in pain?"

"It is no more than I deserve," he looked up at her and for the first time she noticed his eyes. There were no whites in those eyes, they were endless pools of misery, "I told them that I had enough left in me to do this, so there was still a chance for you. They didn't want me to come here all the same. They said they had done it once before and the results of that one were...

mixed."

"What are you talking about, Dad?"

"I don't want you to end up like me. You can't end up like me. The pain!"

The figure opened its mouth impossibly wide and let forth with an ear shattering and blood curdling wail. He wrung his hands. It was the first time Carol had seen anyone wring their hands and mean it and it was terrible to behold. She pushed herself as far up the bed as she could go, scrunching up against the wall.

"Please no!" she protested in the tiniest of voices.

"I can only apologise," said the shade of her father, "this is now my burden and this time you cannot share it."

Carol frowned at this, as it struck a chord in her.

The shade nodded slowly, "we both of us chose to look away from the world and thought that was a good idea, even in the face of the evidence of our own experience. We looked instead into a dark part of ourselves and felt anger and pain. Trouble is, once you start, it's addictive."

The shade took a moment and sat at the end of her bed. She saw him do this and saw the cover of her duvet ruffle, but she felt no discernible weight upon the bed.

He continued, "I thought that I could not stop and because that was what I thought, that was what happened. It's as simple as that. Well, even more simple when you're angry all of the time and you have so much material to feed your anger. I told myself that I was angry at the world and in telling myself that, I had so much reason to be right. The world is a harsh and unfair place. It is cruel and it does not care about you or I."

Carol nodded, for she knew this to be true.

"Oh my child!" said her Dad, and in that moment he sounded so like her Dad it nearly broke her heart, "you nod as if you know this to be the case, but it is the greatest of lies and it is the worst of lies. That it is a lie I told you and a lie that I spent so much time convincing you of is to my eternal shame. And damnation."

"But Dad..." began Carol.

The shade raised a warning hand, "No!" the word was not shouted, but it filled the small room and crashed against her ears, "do not defend me. Instead listen to me. For the sake of your eternal soul and, I may add, the rest of your life in that world we both much maligned."

The shade observed her, as though checking to see if she were listening.

"I was a complete and utter fool. And you are a complete and utter fool. Only, actually, while we're at it, you're making a much better job of that particular foolishness than I ever did, and you're flying in the face of a whole bunch of stuff in order to make your foolishness stick. In fact, that was why they'd written you off. They watch you though, I know they do. They find you *interesting.* I wouldn't be surprised if they didn't put you in their training material, because you stand out."

"Stand out?" Carol was aghast. She stood out? That was the complete opposite of her intended result.

The shade nodded gravely, it was good at nodding gravely. Carol found herself marvelling at this. This was her Dad, it really was, and yet it wasn't. The awful part was that, having revealed his now damned form, he seemed somehow brighter and more full of life than he had at times before his death. How that was possible mystified her, but she knew it to be the case all the same.

"Yes," said her shade-father, "I sold you a lie about looking down making you invisible to the world, didn't I?"

Carol nodded slowly, she really didn't like where any of this was going. She heard the words and she was pretty certain that this *was* her Dad. But these were not her Dad's words all the same.

"I lied!" cried the ghost, "please understand that!"

Another terrible and fearful wail emanated from the ghost and tore through Carol.

"Please stop father!" cried Carol in return.

"I cannot!" wailed the shade, "it is the pain of what I have done, and the frustration at seeing that they were right. I cannot undo all that I have done to you in a single night. I see now, the damage I did to you. They made me see it as part of my punishment. They stripped everything away you see. Everything I had built. The lies and the denial. The huge, thick walls I made so I could avoid the world and worse still the truth. They laid me bare and then they left me until I was ready."

"Did it hurt?" asked Carol meekly.

"I thought it did. At the time, I thought it did. I was so attached to those things. The anger as well. They were what defined me and I was terrified that without those things, I would be nothing."

The shade laughed that cackling laugh of his, "do you want to know the true absurdity of it?"

Carol nodded uncertainly.

"I'd got it all the wrong way around. I was looking in entirely the wrong place. What I thought I hated, I didn't and the things I feared most I made happen."

"What do you mean? Please Dad, tell me what you mean?" Carol's head was a storm of confusion. Her Dad was not making sense to her.

"I feared that I would be nothing without my anger and hate," he cackled again, "and yet it was my anger and hate that made me into nothing. When they tore that away from me, I truly understood that. That if I had let go of my anger and hate in my lifetime then I would have been something. There would have been no stopping that. The lies and denial came with the package. Once my anger was gone, I saw things clearly for what felt like the first time in my life. And then I saw you. They made me look at you and that was when I knew what I had done. I stopped caring about myself a long time ago... no, that in itself is a lie. That is what I said to myself and that is how I acted, but I must have cared only about myself because of the selfish way I acted.

"When I saw you. After they freed me from my hate, and I saw you. I could see what I had done and it was monstrous. I took revenge on the world I hated and I used you to do it. It is the ultimate cowardly act. To use your own child as the weapon of your revenge."

The shade fell into a dark silence, shaking its head as though to dislodge something horrible from inside its skull.

"Why are you saying these things, Dad?" none of it made sense to Carol. These words were not her father's.

"Because I am dead!" shouted the ghost, the words assailing Carol's ears, "you're right, these are not the words of your dear, departed Dad. He can only say them now because he is dead! They find this really funny on the other side. They laugh at our ineptitude. We seldom say what we mean and hardly ever say what we should, thanks to our ridiculous little hang ups. Too embarrassed to make the world a better place. Too proud to say sorry when we know we are wrong and saying sorry would make the world of difference. Too scared to *be* in the world and to live our lives for fear of failure, so instead hiding from life entirely and failing to live at all"

Her Dad stared at her intently as he said those last words, as though awaiting her acceptance. She had no acceptance to give. The ghost nodded at this.

"They were right. I didn't want them to be right, but since when did my refusal to believe something ever make one jot of difference to anyone but me..." he groaned, "...and you."

He looked towards the door, looking even more crestfallen and forlorn than he had throughout this exchange.

"I must go," he said, eyeing the door as though it was the last place he wanted to be, and it was. That was the very nature of purgatory, the last place a person wanted to be, but had to be.

Carol was mostly relieved at this news, albeit with a wee glimmer of sadness at saying goodbye to this version of her Dad, but then, it really wasn't her Dad. She watched as he walked towards the bedroom door to return to whence he came, and Carol found herself willing his interminably slow progress on.

At the door, as she was beginning to feel the first flushes of hope and relief of his departure, he stopped and turned and he waited. Prolonging the moment, as though on purpose.

"Yes," he said, "I am prolonging the moment on purpose. Would a dream do that? No. I am not a product of the cheese you ate..."

He gave her a look right out of her Dad's repertoire of looks and she shrank from the knowledge that he had yet again read her mind and this time her rationalisation of what was happening to her.

"I am not the last visitation you will have this night, child. There will be three more..."

Carol rolled her eyes at this.

"What?" said the ghost of her Dad.

"Really?" said Carol.

Her ghost-Dad shook his head.

"Let me guess, the ghost of Carol past, the ghost of Carol present and the ghost of Carol future?!"

The shade shimmered and changed its hue for a second, a burst of energy changing it in that moment, only for it to return to its sombre grey.

"I didn't know I could do that," said her Dad to himself, "now look here young lady, I'll have less of your lip! I don't have to be here. I did this for you. Yeah, too little and too late, but it's all that I have *and* I convinced them to give me a bit of help because they told me you'd be like this, 'like father like daughter' they said, so yeah, you're going to get three visitations and they... ahem... might seem familiar in some respects..."

He gave her a meaningful look, and she could have sworn that there was the fleeting ghost of a smirk on that ghost's face.

"What?" she asked of that mischievous smile.

He tapped his nose in a way that he had done so often in life. He knew something that she didn't and knowledge was power. She thought he'd leave it at that, which was the usual form, but he didn't, maybe not able to resist a final, parting shot.

"They won't be familiar in other respects."

Then he winked, which with those entirely black orbs for eyes was disconcerting, but more so when the wink was a precursor for him winking out of existence forever.

7

S he was relieved to discover that she had been asleep.

She knew this because she was awakening from that very sleep.

Momentarily, this allowed her to begin the easy work of dismissing the strange cheese dream she'd had about a version of her father that, when she thought about it was right out of her mother's book.

That was it!

Her mother's surprise attack upon her and an unwanted conversation foisted upon her had manifested itself into a dream with the help of a block of cheese that was well past its sell by date. As side effects from consuming food way past its best went, it wasn't a bad one and Carol held onto the underlying elation she'd felt at seeing her Dad once again.

She would have held onto it for a wee while longer had not someone been holding onto the sleeve of her nightdress and tugging her into wakefulness. Still, she tried to hold onto a state of at least sleepiness if not sleep, but the tugger was persistent and insistent in equal measure.

"What!" she cried, even before opening her eyes, begrudging every second of wakefulness to whoever had found their way into her bedroom and...

A number of thoughts smashed into her newly conscious state. Thoughts that included the concept of intruders in her bedroom and how they had got there. Danger! One thought was just that. Danger! It made itself known repeatedly as others jostled for position alongside it.

They all froze in spot, as did she, as the message from her freshly opened eyes arrived at her brain and trumped all else.

There, at the side of her bed, was a little girl.

Of all the things Carol had expected to see, this was not even on her list, let alone down in the nether regions of any list she might have compiled. Even if she had compiled a list and should she have written a word that equated to child or young person or the like, the presence at her bedside at this very moment would still have circumvented all attempts at expectation because child was what she looked like, but child she certainly wasn't.

The huge manga drawn eyes were the first giveaway. Not only the size of the eyes, but the amber colouring that drew all of your attention and did strange and wonderful things to your insides without even asking for permission or consent.

That should have been enough to explain how this child like thing was not a child, but there was more. Another was that she was perfectly symmetrical. How did Carol even consciously know that? That she did was a part of the wonder of this presence. Her skin was flawless, and it wasn't skin by the generally accepted terms humans may agree to generally accept. You could tell that just by looking and Carol had this irresistible compulsion to touch the skin that was almost hypnotically irresistible.

So she did.

She reached out with a determined effort and she touched the skin on the back of the child's hand, it was like nothing she had experienced ever before.

Lifting the hand from her sleeve, she spoke without the reverence she should have felt in the presence of such a being. This was not to say she did not feel that reverence, it was just that she was really good at denying her feelings and masking them too.

"You can stop that for starters," she said as she gave the supernatural being a dark look.

Nothing else occurred for what felt like quite a long time.

In this pause pregnant with all sorts of meaning, knowledge was imparted and this knowledge concerned the form that had manifested itself at Carol's bedside.

They say that man sees perfection in terms limited by his own form. God is a man, only perfect. Hence Jesus coming to earth as the son of God and in being the son of God he *was* God.

Another *they* have questioned this and proposed an alternate view of the universe and it's deity as being a perfect woman. The logic here is that women are already a step up the rung of the ladder to perfection, so God herself must be a woman, her womb the font of all life. That she sent her only begotten son down to Earth in an effort to be more gender inclusive is further proof of the matter.

The They. The *They Who Count,* shake their heads at all of this and yet again wonder at the inhabitants of this planet Earth and their strange and contrary ways. If there were to be any image appropriated from those physically available then the only image that would fit the bill would be that of a child.

Children are perfection personified and it is only the inept and woeful input from adults that veers them tragically away from that perfection. This is so obvious that The They sometimes make noises about giving up on humans altogether and moving somewhere where there are beings intelligent enough to attain the necessary level of self-awareness to make a decent stab at being kind to each other on a consistent and meaningful basis.

Right now, The They were shaking their heads because the child of perfection personified was not a girl. Honestly, put long blond hair on an androgynous child and humans had to go jumping to incorrect and unnecessary conclusions. If The They had not got the patience of saints and some more on top, then this whole thing was in danger of being called off right now.

Luckily for Carol, she was indulged yet again and the pregnant pause came to an end, because she ended it.

"Don't tell me. You're the first of my three visitations," she said this in a huffy monotone.

"OK!" said the first visitation.

"OK, what?" said Carol.

"I won't tell you that I am your first visitation, although technically I'm your second of four."

Carol's brow had knotted at the child's first word, then it had knotted all the more tightly as the child spoke further.

"Your voice?" she ventured.

"Yes?" said the child in the most manly Brummie accent Carol had ever heard.

"Is that really your voice?" she asked the diminutive being with what sounded like a building site foreman's voice. A foreman with a significant smoking habit at that.

"That's a bit subjective. Would you like a different voice?"

"Yes," said Carol.

"How about this?" asked the child using the voice of a famous actress who had specialised in roles as dark, foreboding figures who terrorised children.

"Still creepy," said Carol, giving a shudder to emphasise how she felt about this voice.

"How about..." began the strange cherub at Carol's bedside.

"No!" interrupted Carol, hearing enough of the third voice not to like it one bit, "look, why don't you just use your own voice, OK?"

Now Carol had made an assumption here and this may not have panned out at all well for her, for if the child-being's own voice had not been suitable it would have caused great offence should she have noted this and asked for something else instead.

The child shrugged, "OK, we can do that if you wish."

"Isn't..." began Carol, but she decided this was best left well alone. The child had adopted what it saw as its own voice and if Michael Gambon also happened to have that same voice, then fair enough. There must only be so many voices to go around and some duplication was inevitable.

The child looked askance, but Carol let it be, if Dumbledore had left Hogwarts to narrate whatever this was she was about to embark upon, then that was fine by her, she wasn't going to twist, she'd stick with what was quite a good result, albeit it weird coming from the mouth of this little being.

The child nodded and raised a hand to Carol, its meaning was clear. She was to get out of her bed and follow. Carol pivoted on her bottom and sat up at the side of the bed. She reached out and down at the hand as she took to her feet, readying herself to leave the bedroom.

And then she fell over.

"What was that!?" she exclaimed, rubbing her head despite the fact that she had not hit her head and it had not received any physical injury.

The reason for her exclamation and head rubbing was clear. It surrounded her even now. One moment she had been in her bedroom, the next she was somewhere completely different. No, that wasn't quite right. She was...

"I know this place!" Carol exclaimed again, only now getting over the blur and sudden rushing feeling that had been the effect of her transportation to this place.

The child said nothing, but looked up at her with those big eyes. Eyes that were pleading. A finger went to the lips on that face and the meaning was clear: please shut up!

"Ah," said Carol, and she did her best to shut up.

Which was difficult because having recognised where she was, she turned to the bed that she had slept in in her very earliest years and she let out with quite a loud gasp, for there in her bed was her. Only a version of her that was even smaller than her child companion and that was very disconcerting indeed, especially when the small version of her looked right at her immediately Carol had given forth of that gasp of hers.

Carol's (the larger version) eyes went wide and, remembering herself, she stooped to whisper, "can she see us?"

The child shook its head and again put its finger to its lips.

Maybe the child could hear her, thought Carol, completely missing the point which was that she were to be quiet and listen carefully.

There were voices downstairs. One of them louder than the other. It wasn't an argument as such, more that someone was getting their point across. That someone was Nana. Carol remembered this night all too well and she had always wondered what the two adults downstairs were saying...

"You know," whispered Carol, "I always..."

8

Carol had always wondered what had happened down-stairs and what had been said before her Nana had burst into her room and her Dad had loped in behind her like a chastened, naughty school boy.

There was a whooshing feeling and Carol had the presence of mind to brace herself this time, stumbling but not falling. She made a point of scowling at the child. The child only presented her with a face of innocence. Carol suspected that this face was deployed quite often and was successful in getting the child out of a lot of trouble. This child was, at the very least mischievous and Carol wondered whether it may not be capable of taking things to a level beyond mischief.

The child's attention switched from Carol to the two adults in the room that they had just now whooshed to. Carol was interested to note that they had also come in at the beginning of the conversation, so she wasn't going to miss out on any of it.

"You have to!" Nana said sternly.

Nana was good at stern. Some old ladies were. Carol guessed that they had had many years to perfect this.

"But..." that was her Dad.

Dad was at the dining table and Nana was standing over him. Her positioning added to the stern, Carol thought that she could have been watching a masterclass of stern, but as the scene unfolded she'd realise it was a masterclass of a different sort.

"No! You have got to do it now!" barked her Nana.

Her Dad sighed a heartfelt sigh, "but she's in bed..."

"You might not get another chance, do it while that bitch isn't here or you'll lose your daughter. Do you want that? Because I certainly don't want to lose my granddaughter!"

Her Dad had winced at Nana's use of bitch, this surprised Carol, because she remembered what happened on this night and the complete and utter conviction of the two adults. She had never been privy to this part of the night though, but having wondered what they had said before coming to her bedroom and thought about it, she had guessed that it was more of the same.

"She's not a bitch, Mum. These things happen. She's already said that she wants to do right by me..."

"Right? Right! You wouldn't be getting divorced if she wanted to do right by you! Don't trust a word that that woman says. I know women like her. They tell you whatever you want to hear, but as soon as your back is turned they stick a knife into it. Don't you forget that! And don't you forget that she has all the cards. She could take Carol away from you in a heartbeat and what would that do to you, eh!?"

Her Dad looked incredibly sad as Nana leant over him.

"Exactly!" Nana trilled, "it would be the breaking of you. And if you are ever broken, there'll be no fixing you!"

Her Dad looked up at his mother and Carol saw that sadness change into something else, "I don't want to lose my daughter," he said darkly.

"Good," said her Nana, "then we go up there and we make sure she knows exactly what her mother is like and we make sure that she chooses you right now. We have to make her choose right now. We have to get there before her mother does or else you're in a whole heap of trouble and that bitch will lead you a merry dance. Just you remember what's at stake here and who's created this mess."

Nana seemed to grow larger as she leaned in over her Dad.

Her Dad seemed to shrink from her, but he nodded his acceptance.

"Good, because you sure as hell did nothing to cause this unholy mess, did you?!"

Carol saw a flicker of doubt cross her Dad's face, saw his eyes roll away from the face of his mother. He had had a part in this! She saw it right there and then and that split second was a revelation to Carol, she'd always thought...

...no, she had known. It wasn't just a thought, it was a certainty and yet here she was.

Her Nana was already turning on her heel and heading for the door and the stairs to go to see Carol in her bedroom. Her Nana's blood was up and when her blood was up she was fearsome indeed. There was no stopping her. She could be a venomous old harridan, but she looked after her own and Carol had never been the subject of her anger and particular brand of bile.

"Are you awake, child?" asked her Nana as she walked into the room full of purpose and fierce energy.

The young Carol made a show of sitting up and rubbing her eyes with her balled fists. She had been awake, but she did not want to admit it. She was curious and frightened in equal measure. The older Carol knew all of this. She could remember every word and every moment from this night – but the context of this moment had never before been known to her and she saw it with eyes anew.

"Good," said her Nana as her Dad filed into the small bedroom beside her.

Her Dad's shoulders were slumped and he looked terrible. Not just upset, but crushed under the weight of the world. A more forlorn man Carol had never seen and she remembered her heart going out to him when she was a little girl. Now though, that automatic response had stalled as she watched both him and her Nana with something approaching fascination.

"We've got something important to tell you," said Nana.

Carol nodded gravely, "Mum and Dad are getting a divorce."

"Yes," agreed Nana, "but you need to know a few things about that. Things that your Mum won't tell you, but I will."

Little Carol's face scrunched up, she didn't want to talk about the divorce and already she was feeling desperately uncomfortable.

"First things first, child," said her Nana all business like, "your Dad doesn't want a divorce. It's all your Mum. She's caused all of this unholy mess and she's intent on wrecking your home. What do you think to that?"

Nana stood there leaning towards Carol, expecting an answer.

All Carol could manage was, "I..."

"Hmmm..." said Nana, "take a look at your father! Look at the state he's in! Heartbroken! That woman has broken him and hurt him in ways I hope you'll never be able to imagine! What do you think about that?!"

Carol's face crumpled and a tear ran down her cheek.

"Yes!" said her Nana triumphantly, "your mother has lied and cheated and broken everything that we hold dear. She isn't the woman any of us thought she was! She cannot be trusted! She's poison! She's taken a home full of love and filled it with hate. She is a hateful and untrustworthy creature!"

The watching Carol was finding all of the fire and brimstone hard to stomach. This was all too much. How could anyone say these things to a small child? Surely her mother wasn't that bad? And that was when a worm of doubt found its way into Carol's mind. Perhaps things were not as she thought they had been and if that were the case, then maybe they were not now as she thought they were...?

The worst was yet to come, though. Her Nana had just shattered a little girl's entire world into tiny little pieces, but this was only the opening act, the coup de gras was to follow on the heels of this pitiless onslaught.

"Your Mum and Dad hate each other, child," stated her Nana, "so you have to choose. Look at how hurt your Dad is. Don't you think he needs you now more than he ever has?"

Little Carol nodded carefully as her Dad dutifully played his part.

"Daddy?" said little Carol raising her arms to the only parent she had in what was left of her world right now, her absent mother had been destroyed and in her place was a baleful monster who would become the subject of little Carol's hurt, hate and anger.

Her Dad silently walked to her and gave her a big hug. Over his shoulder she could see Nana. Watching. Expectant.

"Well?" asked her Nana, "who do you choose?"

Carol had no choice, it had to be her Dad, there was no one else available to choose. That she had no choice and was being coerced was not at all obvious to her and never would be. Not unless there was a miracle or supernatural visitation...

"Daddy," she said and with that one word, her entire life was changed. The safe and secure reality she had had had been demolished with her in the very midst of it and in the ensuing trauma she had been forced to embrace this new world where her mother was a treacherous monster and her Dad was a broken thing with a deep well of hurt that she had been invited to share.

Carol could see it now, in being forced to make this choice she had taken on her Dad's pain as her own and she had always felt responsible for that pain, hurt and anger. Responsible for him.

"I don't need to see anymore," said Carol to the child.

The child looked up at her with those huge, inscrutable amber eyes and it took her hand, "there is more to see," it said as they left this place and went on to their next destination.

Which was the kitchen of this very house. The daylight was streaming into the kitchen and there, leaning against the work units opposite each other were her mother and father.

Carol felt uncomfortable seeing them both in the same room. This was, she knew, her Dad's idea of hell. Only it hadn't been. Not back then and not before the divorce.

Her mother was speaking, "Carol has to be our priority. Always and forever. She is the best thing we have ever done and I want her to be OK. OK?"

Her Dad nodded.

"She needs her Dad and she needs her Mum, so everything needs to be fair and even. Whatever happens and however we may feel, we're the grown-ups and we have to do the best for her. Always."

Her Dad nodded again.

"So she'll spend half her time with you and half her time with me and we'll do our best by her to make both our homes as warm and welcoming and good as they can be. I'll never bad mouth you or speak ill off you in front of Carol, Jacob. That's not fair on any of us and certainly not on Carol. I love her with all of my heart and I just want her to come through this and to have a happy childhood and have a chance of a good life."

Emily looked at the silent Jacob, he said nothing but nodded for a third time.

"I know you're hurt, Jacob. So am I. We've tried and we've tried and I'm sorry, I can't go on like this. She needs her Dad though and I'm not going to behave like some parents do. I'm not going to go for any more than half her time, or for more than half of anything for that matter. Carol should never be caught up in our problems or hurt should she?"

"No," said Jacob.

Carol knew that a lot of kids who had gone through divorce spent most of their time with their mothers, seeing their fathers every other weekend. However, even now as an adult, she hadn't equated this to her own life. She didn't realise that by agreeing a fair, half and half split, her mother was actually giving up a proportion of what she was entitled to. Her mother really was trying to do the right thing by Carol, but she had never been allowed to see that.

Whatever Carol's mum did, Carol had been brainwashed into seeing her as the cause of the divorce and all of the resultant hurt. Her mum had *done the wrong thing,* and she was monstrous and not to be trusted.

Emily tried for a smile, "whatever it takes, Jacob. It needs to be fair and equal. She needs both of us and she should never even feel like she has to make a choice between us. That should never be in question. She needs to be as safe and secure as possible in the circumstances."

Carol's mouth was wide open at this exchange, "she doesn't know! He didn't tell her! How could he stand there when she's trying to do the right thing and not even tell her!?"

Carol looked from the child to her parents.

"We have to *do* something!" and as she stepped forward to shake her Dad and demand he confess, the scene blurred.

84

Next, the child, holding Carol's hand gently but firmly, took Carol through a series of scenes. These, she knew, were times before the break up. Times before she was forced to make a choice that was no choice at all.

The scenes alternated between her mother and her Dad. Each of them sad and alone. No longer in a relationship, other than officially, on a slip of paper. Carol saw her Dad behaving exactly how her Dad had always behaved. That he had been like this even before the divorce was another revelation. That his behaviour hurt her mother was not.

She did not blame her Dad, this was just the way he was and the relationship with her mother was destined not to work. That she had blamed, and was still blaming her mother escaped her as she watched two people struggling in a bad situation that could not be sustained, not unless there was compromise and change and her Dad had not changed in all of the years she had known him. Her mother however...

The scenes ended and there was a pause of movement where Carol found herself in her old bedroom. It was empty of her former self, but there was still the presence of the child she had been and the smell of the room that she remembered so well. She felt a nostalgic elation and let herself believe that she could walk from the room and down the stairs to find her parents in the rooms below, one in the kitchen cooking dinner, the other in the living room immersed in a book or a TV program.

This made her think of her memories of the three of them together. She had so few, and yet she had held onto the belief that she had been robbed of a Utopian life by her mother's untrustworthiness and that she should forever more be wary and careful around such an unreliable and terrible person. That this extended to the rest of *that family* that her mother had built around her had not escaped her, but what had was that she had failed to form a single decent relationship with anyone. Including her Dad.

"Why?" was the only word she said as some of the truth of the world sank in.

The child said nothing, but taking her hand again transported her, not back to her own bedroom and welcome sleep as she had expected, but somewhere else entirely.

9

This place was not familiar to Carol, she knew it to be a bedroom, but barring that obvious utility of the room that the bed gave away, there was nothing else that sparked a memory or familiarity to Carol whatsoever.

The door opened, startling Carol. She turned towards the sound and movement in time to see a little boy enter the room. He slunk in, eyes downcast and a slope to his shoulders. He fell onto the bed with a noticeable lack of energy and enthusiasm and he sighed heavily as he looked up at the ceiling. He lay there like that for some while. Silent and unmoving.

"There you are!"

A familiar voice, but a much younger version of Nana. To see Nana as a young woman was strange and oddly magical. In the pause after those three words, she looked pretty and not a bunch of sharp and abrasive edges. The Nana that Carol had known was rough-hewn and pretty was not a word she ever could have associated with her because pretty had a softness to it that Nana just did not have.

When this young Nana spoke though, the prettiness was banished.

"That Barbara has been at it again you know. What a bitch! Not to be trusted..."

This was only the start of a fifteen minute diatribe at the end of which Nana sat on her Dad's bed and ruffled his hair.

"It's just you and me, Jacob. The world is poison and everyone is out to hurt you. Give your Ma a hug and tell her it'll be alright..."

She sat expectantly awaiting Jacob to do as he was told. The smile on her face as she held her son was triumphant and Carol thought a little wicked.

"You're so much more of a man than your Dad, Jacob. You're my boy. You're my world. I sometimes wonder why I ever married that waste of space. At least I have you and these secret chats of ours. What we have is special and not to be shared with anyone. Without you, well I'd just die. You keep me alive, Jacob. If you were ever to leave me I think I'd kill myself."

She held him all the closer then, and Carol could see the little boy's shoulders shuddering up and down in the all too familiar movements of a small child crying. That Nana was grinning as she held the crying child was a terrible sight to behold.

Carol had asked why and this was her answer.

The child took her hand and walked her through times in her Dad's childhood that helped her understand why he was the way he was.

Brainwashed was the word that Carol thought scene after scene, his mother instilling in him his absolute need for her and nothing and no one else. She constantly tore down everyone else in his world so that he had no one else other than her. The way she spoke as well as the words she used were pure poison. Carol was shocked to see that in her younger days, Nana was even more powerful and venomous, that the Nana that she had known had mellowed with age.

How could a mother do this to her son, she thought, and an echo of this question followed closely on its heels: how could a father do this to his daughter?

One person to replace an entire world? That could never be enough, however good that person was. The problem was made all the worse by the fact that anyone capable of this was already damaged goods, so the alternative they presented was badly broken and would result in nothing good whatsoever.

The tableaus of what Carol guessed were her Dad's memories slowed and then froze. Carol smiled at the sad irony of the gift that her Dad had extended her beyond the grave. She had desperately wanted to know her Dad. Had begged and pleaded with him, and then silently wished for him to open up and talk candidly about himself. She had wanted to *know*. To know him and have the promised relationship with him. The carrot that dangled eternally in front of her, having chosen him and having been made to make a choice that was never a choice.

Now she was seeing more of her Dad than she had ever seen in life and she realised that she didn't want it. That he had clung to her desperately, terrified that he was going to lose her and that eventuality was always going to be the only outcome. She had known so little of him and now what she did know was falling apart. The very thing that he had done to her mother was always going to happen to him in the end.

There was a terrible inevitability to it.

"You reap what you sow," Carol said under breath.

And now she was back in her bedroom, stood by her bedside facing the small, angelic child.

Without thinking she sat heavily on her bed.

"I am so exhausted," she gasped, "that is all too much. I don't know what I am to do with what you have shown me, and I don't know why you have shown me these things. To shock me? To hurt me so soon after the death of the only person I have ever loved? You leave me with nothing."

Carol shook her head, overwhelmed and feeling very sorry for herself. Tired, she thought, I am so tired.

"Not nothing," said the voice of Michael Gambon from the mouth of the small child.

90

This jolted Carol to a more wakeful state. The child had not spoken during their travels and she had forgotten about the strange voice of the small creature, but there it was and the child-being had her full attention now.

"You have two more visitations to come this night."

Carol pulled a face of puzzlement and snatched up her watch from the bedside table to see that it was only a minute to 1am. She hadn't been tracking time prior to this, but still, all of that had happened in such a short frame of time. The thought of it made her head hurt.

"But..." she began, realising that she was talking to the thin air and there was only her in the bedroom.

She flung herself back on the bed, watch still in her hand and after only a moment of ceiling gazing her eyes flickered shut and she was fast asleep.

10

"Pull my finger," she was saying to someone in the Falcon as she extended said finger over the bar.

They looked at the finger as though it were an alien object.

"Go on, pull my finger," she said again, smiling.

The bar fly shrugged and wrapped a tiny, little hand delicately around her finger and pulled ever so gently.

Aghast, Carol looked upon the tiny appendage that emanated from the overlarge sleeve. The juxtaposition of tiny hand with large, hairy professional alcoholic was unholy.

The punter tugged genteelly on her finger again.

And again.

What the..?!

Through one sleep encrusted eye, Carol observed the child-being pulling on her finger to awaken her. As dreams went, dreaming she was being awoken from a dream by a mythical creature was out there. She doubted she'd find a dream analysis for this when she looked it up in the morning and recounting this night's dreams with anyone would be a risky business indeed. The listener would think Carol had taken leave of all of her senses.

"Oh, it's you again..."

Despite her unwillingness to be roused from sleep, she sat up and moved around to sitting. Noticing her discarded watch on the pillow she picked it up to place it on the bedside table. As she did, she spotted the time.

"1am!?" she bellowed, "you gave me all of a minute!"

"We're on a tight schedule," said the little mite. In the voice of... who was that? Emma Thompson?

Carol was going to continue with her protest, but again, if she were going to have a dream narrated then, there were few better options, if any. There were certainly many worse options. In her tired state she found her mind wandering almost deliriously through some of those options including the braying laugh of a slightly controversial comedian. Yes, there were worse options. She wondered what the third option would be, then decided not to think about it. What would be, would be.

"I thought I was getting three different visitations tonight?"

asked Carol.

"You are," confirmed the child in the voice of Emma.

Carol tried not to think of Nanny McPhee.

"You're not different, you're just using Emma Thompson's voice."

"Who?"

Carol pulled an incredulous face and then let that one go, "you're the same baby aren't you?"

"I'm..!" exclaimed the small child, "I am not a baby!"

"Aha!" exclaimed Carol right back at the child, "you are the same child-thing thought aren't you? I even caught a hint of Gambon in there!"

"Who?"

"Really? Thompson? Gambon?"

"Never heard of them."

"OK," sighed Carol, "but you're not telling me you're not the same child, only using a different voice."

"I am."

94

"But you're not."

"Why would you even say that?!"

"Because you look exactly the same!"

"I take exception to that. I think you're being a bit cherubist and I'm deeply offended."

"Because you look exactly the same as the last visitation?"

"Yes. That. I can't help it if perfection personified looks like this. I mean, you can't add to perfection or take away from it can you? Ergo, you cannot change it can you?" the child-being looked at her with wide and expectant amber eyes.

Carol rolled her own eyes in response, "OK, let's get this visit over, Emma."

"Emma?" asked the child in the voice of Emma Thompson.

"Never mind," said Carol, extending her hand to the child and awaiting her conveyance to another time and another place.

Nothing happened.

"Erm...?" said Carol.

"This visitation is to the present," explained the mini depiction of perfection.

Carol looked around the bedroom, "right."

Then she made up her mind. She may as well go with this and get it over. So she stood up and walked out of her bedroom and downstairs. She walked into the kitchen and looked around at the familiar units and the cooker and the stainless steel sink. This was a kitchen. Her kitchen.

The child walked in, well waddled in, thought Carol.

"Oy!" said the child.

"What?" said Carol.

"Waddled! That's not nice!"

"Oh. You heard that?"

The child nodded and folded its arms, looking at her expectantly.

"Sorry," she said, feeling a little ashamed that she'd been rude to a small child. That was a bit low.

She made a show of looking around the kitchen again, "well? What's next?" she asked in an attempt to prompt something of interest.

"This," said the child.

And with that, a wave of light came in from the window and a ghost of Carol strobed in and around the kitchen. The light waned and grew again and again and the faint version of Carol strobed around industriously. She walked from the kitchen to the living room to observe the same thing. A crazy bee version of Carol moving in and out of the room.

Up in the bedroom, the rapidly moving Carol went back and to and back and to to such an extent that the observing Carol could have sworn a groove would appear in the exact spot of floor she always seemed to use.

"What is this?" Carol asked the child after a while.

"Your life," said the child simply.

Carol frowned, "really?"

"Yes, really," confirmed the child.

"But I don't see..." began Carol.

"Anyone else?" supplied the child.

"Oh..." said Carol, now beginning to see.

"Anything else?" supplied the child again.

"There are books," protested Carol.

"And..?" asked the child.

"I think I preferred the first visitation," grumbled Carol, "she was silent for most of that visit."

"I am not a she!" cried the child.

"Aha! Busted! You are just the one strange child!"

"Perfection personified!" corrected the perfection personified child.

"And what was the minute all about?"

"Union rules. I have to take a break," explained the child.

Carol shook her head and rolled her eyes, "Right. Well, what next?"

The child shrugged.

"You're telling me this is it? This is all I am doing with my life?" grizzled Carol.

The child cautiously reached out and took her hand.

* * *

"You're telling me that's it? That that is all she is doing with her life!?"

Similar words, and yet another voice. This time it was Bob's.

He was sat at the dining room table in the home he shared with her mother. She was also there, sat hunched over a steaming mug of tea. The full complement of that family was there in that moment, with Timmy sat with his own mug of tea, observing the current exchange. He still had his own personal mug at his parent's house even having moved out to his own, bigger house several years ago. The trade in exotic cars having served him well.

Carol wondered whether her own mug, the one with a witch on a broomstick that she'd chosen on a family shopping expedition was still there, in this house. She found that she was hoping that it still was.

The cherubic personage opened the mug cupboard and pointed at the very mug she had been thinking of and it winked an overlarge eye at her. She shook her head and rolled her eyes again. Now inexplicably annoyed at the presence of that mug and also annoyed at the really annoying child.

"What can we do, Bob?" her mother sounded so sad and the sound of it captured Carol's attention again.

This seemed to have an effect on her step-Dad and he half sat, half fell into his own chair. The three of them sat quietly for a moment. The silence a heavy and terrible thing between them. She knew that she was the cause of that silence. That she *was* that silence, and being in the room and experiencing this had a surreal quality to it.

"I'm sorry," said Bob, a sadness in his voice now as well, "I didn't mean to sound ranty. I just feel so helpless. I... she had so much potential. Such a beautiful child..."

"She still does and she still is," said her Mum.

"Yes, I know. It's just... she's wasting it. It's like she's trapped in a way of being that she just can't see. I thought that when she left the area she would find... I dunno...something... or failing that, someone... but she came back and even though Jacob has gone, it's like his hold over her hasn't. If anything it's got worse since her died and she has too."

Emily looked up at Bob, tears streaming down her face, they reached hands out to each other, grasping and squeezing. With his free hand, he stroked the hand he held and Bob consoled his wife, "don't cry love, you have always done your very best. You've given everything you have."

"Then why do I feel like I failed?"

Her mother looked old in that moment, like the years had all caught up with her. Carol thought that she didn't look like she had much life left in her at all.

"It was me who failed," said Bob sadly, "she's hated being here ever since we got together and bought this place."

"She was like that before you came along. The divorce affected her badly," said Emily.

"But she's hated me from the outset. I think I gave her a focus for that hate."

"Stop it!"

This was a new voice. Not just Timmy speaking for the first time, but Timmy speaking in a way that Carol had not heard before.

"Stop it both of you! Neither of you deserve this. This is all on her. She *chose* to be that way. She is still choosing to be that way. You have both done more than your best by her. You've sacrificed so much and she's never appreciated any of it. Welcoming her into your home even when each and every time she brought hate with her. We all knew it. But you never gave in. Not once. The time and the effort! No wonder it's taken its toll! I know it's taken its toll on me! I missed out on so much. I sometimes wonder what life would have been like if you'd both given me half of your available time..."

"Timmy... I..." Bob stuttered these words, shocked at the unexpected outburst.

"We... I thought..." began Emily.

"No. No you didn't. You didn't think at all. It's as much my fault as anyone's. I made it easy. Good old Timmy, always happy and smiley! I sat on the side lines and I willed you to succeed. I was invested as you both were. But I knew in my heart of hearts that you couldn't win."

"Why!?" gasped Emily.

"Because I could see! Carol never once let go of whatever it was she brought here. She never once relaxed or tried to be a part of this family or this home. Do you know what? I offered her the chance to come in as a partner of my business, or anything really. Come and speak to me and we'll work something out. I just wanted her to come and see me. Make an effort. She's blanked me entirely. It's as though I'm not a part of her life. That we're not brother and sister." He sighed and shrugged his shoulders, "I just wanted to see my big sister. So even though I could see you guys were onto a loser, I did the exact same thing and hoped against hope that she would come good. And she hasn't."

Timmy, looked completely deflated and the sight of it made Carol feel overwhelmingly sad and awful. She had a momentary urge to go to him and hug him and she felt an even larger wave of sadness as she realised that she couldn't because he couldn't see or feel her there, but worse still, that if she had been in the room for real, she wouldn't and couldn't have brought herself to console her brother and that that barrier between them was entirely of her own making.

Well, of her Nana's making.

And of her Dad's making.

But they were now both dead and gone and yet that ridiculous and terrible barrier remained.

She looked around the table at the three people in the world who had always, always loved her unconditionally and only ever wanted her to be a part of this family and this home and she saw what she had done to them. She could see that they had no more fuel left in the tank. They'd given it everything they had.

Right now, it looked like Carol had won and this was what her victory looked like. If this was her prize, then she did not want it.

Even now, if she were to get on a bus or order a taxi, she could be here in a matter of minutes and she could start to make it alright. She knew that they would welcome her with open arms. She couldn't see herself here though. She could not visualise herself in this room with these people because she had held something of herself back each and every time she had been in this house for fear of betraying the choice she had been forced to make all those years ago.

"Is there anything else you need to show me?" she asked the child wanting to leave this place now.

11

A nd now she is outside, at the front door of the house she was in only a second ago.

That door.

And although this is the second visitation and this visitation is of the present, her present, she is taken back in time to the very first day she encountered this door and she knows that this door has always held this challenge for her.

This is the door to her other home. Her treacherous and untrustworthy mother's lair. Her mother who had compounded her treachery by making real her displacement of her Dad by marrying another man and so preventing a return to happiness for her Dad, and trapping Carol in an anguished limbo ever since.

Then they made matters even worse by having a perfect child, a child that looks very like the child that has visited twice already tonight and is standing beside her right now.

Perfection personified.

11

The door.

Every time she is confronted by this door it asks its question of her.

Will you betray your Dad?

And having asked its question, it waits. It waits knowing that Carol is terrified. That she does not want this door to open and for her to be found lacking by her father.

Even now, after all these years and in the relative safety of her dream state those self-same raw feelings bubble up within her. She is terrified and in that terror there is confusion.

How can she be here in this place?

Who can she be here in this place?

For she cannot be herself. In being herself there is the very real danger that she will relax even if for a moment, and in that moment she will enjoy herself and that will be a betrayal.

The Betrayal.

And her Dad will *know.* Because her Dad has been betrayed before, and he was betrayed by the woman who lives in this place. Carol cannot afford to be like that woman. She cannot afford to like that woman.

Her Dad has been active ever since Nana's visit to her bedroom.

105

Daily he has reminded her of the choice she made. She is under no illusion, if she were to fail, bad things would happen. If she were to even hint at any of this then she will have failed and he will *know*.

He is a quiet man, but the threat is clear and ever present, made all the more sinister by that dark, brooding quiet. Her Dad remains a dark, angry and hateful man.

So, she has to pretend. For half of her life she has to pretend to be someone that she isn't and somewhere along the way she loses herself as she hides from this world. She does not know who she is anymore. She brings hate from her Dad's house to her mother's house. She carries that hate and it's anger with her always. This is the burden she was made to carry when she was forced to make that choice. It is terrible and it is hers. There is nothing that can be done about it because she can never tell her mother because bad things would happen if she did.

Besides, her Nana killed that mother on the fateful night she forced the choice upon her, so she has no one to turn to. Other than her Dad, and her Dad will not help her here.

The door looms up, impossibly large and foreboding and it asks its question and challenges her once again. She beats a hand against it and cries "no!" and once she does, the hand becomes a fist and hits against that door again and again and again and she is crying, "No!"

"No!"

"NO!"

12

"**N**o!"

"NO!"

She is sobbing as she pummels her pillow.

On all fours, her body wracked by those sobs as she hits out again and again.

Through her tears and her protestations she hears a gentle clearing of a throat.

"Erm...?" says another familiar voice. "Excuse me?"

Ricky Gervais. It is the voice of Ricky Gervais. Of course it is. This is somehow fitting.

Carol turns her head towards the sound of the voice and as she does she draws in a laboured breath. Then she gasps.

"What happened to you?!"

The child pulls a face at her. She supposes it is a scowl, but it looks more like a baby with trapped wind.

"You're grey!" she exclaims.

"Yes, well..." says the grey child in the voice of Ricky Gervais.

"Why are you grey?" she asks as she frees herself of the duvet and sits before him.

"Because I'm the third visitation?"

"What, and you had to paint yourself grey because that's the colour of a future visitation?"

Carol was quite proud of the way she summed up her theory.

But the small child shook it's head, "did you notice the colour of your Dad?" it asked.

"Yes, he was grey like you..." said Carol, uncertainty creeping into her voice.

The child nodded in grim fashion.

A dawning realisation fell upon Carol and roughed her up, "you're grey because my future is grim."

"What future," said the child nonchalantly.

"Hey!?" gasped Carol.

The child shook its head dismissively, "look, I've seen your future and if I were you, I just wouldn't bother. Actually living it the once will be bad enough, you don't want to make it any worse."

"Surely it's not that bad?" asked Carol.

"No. It's not bad..." said the child.

Carol hadn't finished letting out her breath of relief when the child spoke again.

"It's much worse than that..."

Carol braced herself for transportation into the future in any case. The way the child had spoken told her that they were about to do that whooshing thing that happened between the places that they visited. She closed her eyes and awaited the moment.

"Erm..." said the child, "what are you doing?"

"Bracing myself for my future," explained Carol, her eyes remaining firmly shut.

"So you really want to do this?" said the child.

"Yes," said Carol quite certainly.

"Only I was hoping to knock off early and it takes ages to get rid of all this grey."

Carol opened her eyes and eyed the child, "that's make up?"

The child looked uncomfortable, "no," it said in a small and somewhat unconvincing voice.

She licked her finger and wiped it along the child's forearm. She was disappointed that there was no resultant smearage.

"Oy! What's your game!?" said the child as it recoiled and hopped away comically.

Carol supressed a laugh, "I wanted to know whether it's make up," she explained.

"Well it's not," said the child.

"What is it then?"

"It's dread pigment," sighed the child.

"Dread pigment?" asked Carol, having never heard of the stuff.

"Yeah, it's like the stuff auras are made of, only it permeates the skin."

"Right," said Carol in that way that conveys some degree of not understanding.

"Look," said the child, "you know when you can see that someone is down and sad and really suffering?"

"Yes," said Carol.

"Well grey is the colour of all of that."

"OK."

"It's the shadow of all the darkness that a person is harbouring and a dire warning to others not to go where that person has gone."

"Because they've turned to the dark side?"

"Yes, and the darkness is leaking out of them."

"So you want me to use the force and be a good Jedi?"

"Eh? What?" the child shook its head, "you're not taking any of this seriously are you? Cripes lummee! They said that you were a lost cause, but I thought that was management speak. Here, give me your hand, let's get this over with. I have a box set and a packet of Jaffa cakes with my name on waiting for me after this. Honestly, you people, you don't know when you have it good. You just have to take it all for granted, look in completely the wrong direction and screw it all up. And then you moan about the world not being fair and how bad your lot is. It's a travesty is what it is..."

There was a whooshing, that if it wasn't quite as whooshy, Carol would have gotten used to by now. As it was, she was quite pleased that she only wobbled and managed to stay standing this time.

"...Star Wars references. I mean that's taking the Michael isn't it? I'm not even being paid for this last one. One minute they're giving it the solemn speech about lost causes and the next they're telling me that you probably won't even need the third visitation, just a quick word about how dreadful the future is. That'll get the message across, is what they said. Don't make me laugh. I mean look at you! You've not listened to a word I've..."

The child looked up at Carol and saw that it was exactly on the money. Carol had indeed not been listening to a word it had said.

"What is this?" asked Carol in a small voice.

The child sighed, "the future?" it said this in a haughty manner that teenagers manage to perfect in no time at all. One day they are pleasant children. The next day this stroppy way of speaking happens along with a bunch of other inexplicable stuff that defies explanation and is beyond the help of even cherubic visitations.

"It's very dark," said Carol, as she stared out into the sort of darkness that you could mine, it was that tangible.

"Yeah, well..." began the child, thinking that it had warned her about this future and what else did she expect?

Carol's brow creased, "is there something in there?"

She didn't await an answer from the child and it was a good job too as the child was feeling somewhat aggrieved and had its arms firmly crossed. It trailed behind her in a huff as she walked carefully towards the movement that she had spotted.

The walk felt long and arduous, and yet it was over in a matter of seconds. There before her, shrouded in the ominous darkness was a scene she did not want to witness.

"Not this," she said quietly, "anything but this."

The child remained silent this time because there was nothing left to say. Whether Carol accepted the scene presented to her or not was irrelevant. Acceptance was her choice and it didn't change a thing. Other than her.

On shaking legs, she edged nearer to the graveside scene.

There was a crowd here. Many of the faces familiar. This was a mild surprise as she hadn't realised she knew so many people, and not so many that would all gather in one place. That these faces were here could mean only one thing.

She knew the person who was being put in the ground and it could be only one of two people, and she *knew* that it was her mother before she took another step and was able to see the gravestone.

At the grave's edge were Bob and Timmy. Timmy had an arm wrapped around his father. They're roles seemingly reversed in this moment. Bob seemed to have shrunk into himself. He was crying. Witnessing those tears was the hardest thing to endure for Carol. That hit her harder than the fact of her mother's death. Those tears were what her mother's death meant and Bob was so close to the grave's edge that Carol could see them fall down and down, each of them landing on the lid of her mother's coffin.

She drew in a stertorous breath and scanned the mourners another time.

"There it is," said the child, "she's got it..."

Carol put it down to the shock discovery of her mother's death and the harsh reality presented to her. In her confusion she had assumed that she was there, present at the funeral, because she was most definitely here witnessing it right now.

But of course, this was a vision that she was not a part of and it was only now that she understood that she was not here at the funeral. She was not amongst the mourners of her own mother's funeral.

"Why am I not here, child?" she said with trembling lips, "am I... also dead?"

The child sighed.

"What is it?" asked Carol.

The child sighed an even bigger sigh, "Yes. In a manner of speaking you are."

"I am what?" said Carol.

"Dead," said the child, not putting a finer point on it.

"But.." began Carol.

Whoosh.

She had barely registered the child reaching out and taking her hand. Now she was in the familiar environs of her kitchen. That horrible darkness pressing in from all around her.

She watches as another version of her, one that does not look that much older than her, but that has an aged and bitter look to her features opens an envelope and, barely taking a moment to read it, tosses the card inside onto the kitchen table.

The card is the funeral invitation. Carol has always found that odd. Invitations are for parties and the good things in life and yet she knows no other way to describe the card that sits there on the table, barely touched and obviously unobserved.

Then they are in the living room at the exact same time that her mother's funeral is taking place. This version of her sits on the sofa and reads a book. The book is a book about a world where magic is the predominant force and the players in this story have powers. They can be so much more than dull and boring people via the use of magic. Carol has chosen to escape the world whilst the woman who bore her, brought her into the world and loved her with all her heart each and every day she lived in this world is put to rest.

There are no goodbyes from this Carol, as far as she is concerned, she said her goodbyes a long, long time ago and there is nothing

116

further to be said and certainly no more to be done.

The ominous and cloying darkness closes in slowly but surely and the reading Carol is oblivious as she is swallowed up and taken away.

When the darkness opens up again, a disoriented Carol is back at the graveyard.

"But we've already been here," Carol says to the child.

The child does not speak, it points solemnly towards a solitary figure by an open grave.

Timmy stands there in the drizzle. The funeral is over, but he remains. He hasn't finished and he has more to say to his dear, departed parent.

Carol draws nearer in an effort to hear more clearly what he is saying. As she nears the grave, she realises that this is not a return to her mother's grave. This is Bob's grave, only they share the same plot. As she reads the grave stone, she sees that Bob survived her mother by only six months. The year of their deaths is shockingly close to the present year. Despite her Dad's death, Carol has not considered her mother's mortality. This is too soon and they are too young.

Still she fails to catch the quiet words Timmy is saying to his deceased parents, but that he is conversing with them is clear. She knows that she hasn't attended this funeral, that if she failed to attend her mother's funeral than there was no way she could bring herself to come to Bob's.

A second figure approaches Timmy and wraps an arm around him.

"Come in from the rain, love. You're soaked," the woman's voice is soft, warm and reassuring and there is much love there.

Timmy, it appears, has found the time from his business and his friends to get married. Carol wonders whether he is married already, if not, he is surely dating this woman and yet Carol has never met her. Of course she hasn't. She has precious little to do with her half-brother. What pains her the most is the thought that Timmy may have actively kept this woman from Carol. Is he ashamed of her now?

Carol follows the two of them as they walk back to the large black car waiting to take them to the wake. Inside, they join two very small children, a girl and a boy. The resemblance the kids have to Timmy and herself is striking and she feels a moment of inexplicable joy to see them for the first ever time.

"She should have been here," Timmy's voice trembles with something like anger.

"You knew that she would not come," says his wife.

"She's the reason they both died like this!" growled Timmy.

Carol had never, ever seen him like this and she hadn't heard him say a bad word about anyone in his life. He was always so impossibly happy and bright, this version of him was shocking and appalling.

"Timmy, you can't talk like this," cautioned his wife.

No, agreed Carol soundlessly, you can't...

"I'm only speaking the truth. You don't know. You weren't there. She could have been anything. She had so much potential. And I don't mean a rocket scientist or a Nobel prize winner, although she was very, very bright. But she had this light inside her and when she forgot herself and *was* herself, she was a joy to behold. That happened less and less though. I saw it happen in those early days you know. She'd be laughing and full of joy and then it were as though she remembered something and she just stopped and she went cold. It was horrible. Like a switch was flicked and the shutters came down. And that coldness, it was hate."

"She sound like a damaged person," said Timmy's wife.

"Yeah, but I've never understood why! Our Folks gave us both so much love and made a point of spending loads of time with us. They told us so much. It was never a case of No! Stop! Or anything like that. Of course they told us off, but they treated us with respect and explained things to us and they kept on and on about never closing doors and wanting us to have a such a wide appreciation of things that we would have the world at our feet. That we should have as many choices as possible because that way we could find a life that energised and fulfilled us."

"Well, it worked for you didn't it?" his wife smiled warmly.

Timmy returned that smile and his face lit up, Carol saw the little boy she had grown up with and it lit her up as well.

"It didn't work for Carol though," as he said her name his face darkened and the joyous little boy was banished from that moment, "she made one choice and it was a really bad one." He sighed deeply and looked at his two children, "she's never seen either of the children. Hasn't acknowledged the existence of her niece and nephew. I mean what kind of a person does that?"

Timmy's wife squeezed his hand, choosing not to answer and leave it as a rhetorical question.

"She broke their hearts, Meg. I saw both of them go downhill as they realised that she was lost to them. That she would choose to be alone in the world rather than ever darken their door, and once Mum died, Dad was lost. It was bloody terrible. I wanted to be enough for them, but I couldn't be and I couldn't fix it either. Carol may be damaged, but she broke them and she neither knows, nor cares."

Carol wants to say something to her grieving brother, but as she opens her mouth to speak the darkness closes in again and Carol feels it all the more, having seen her brother and witnessed his anguish and the bitterness that he feels towards her. She knows that he is not built like that and that he deserves better.

As the darkness dissipates, it does not draw back anywhere near as much as it has previously. She struggles to see what it is that is before her. Directly before her, at a short distance is a grey slab. The disorienting darkness scrambles her thoughts and she takes a while to discern it for what it is.

Of course it is.

Things some in threes, and this is another gravestone.

"What does it say?" she asks into the darkness, a darkness so thick and cloying that she can no longer see the child.

In response to her question, an eerie luminescence lights up the engraving on the stone slab, character by character.

She sees her name gradually revealed by the unnatural light, and then the legend...

Died Alone

She gasps and points towards the stone, "what is this!?"

But she knows there will be no further response.

This visitation is not done with her yet, for between her and her gravestone is the open grave. As her awareness of this open grave makes itself known in her consciousness, her gaze lowers and she peers down into the dark.

If she thought that the darkness surrounding her was ominous, she was wrong. The darkness she now stares down into is absolute. It is elemental.

It is the abyss.

As she stares into it, she knows that this is not the first time that she has stared into this darkness. This is where she goes when she attempts to escape the world she so hates. That her hatred of that world is misplaced and all her hate has ever been of is herself. She hates herself and this is where her hate takes her.

To the dark.

And there is a power to this darkness that will not be denied. She feels its draw. It pulls her towards it and she cannot resist. She forms her lips to say no, but the word never forms and silently she falls forwards and down into the grave and into the abyss.

Falling.

Falling.

Lost.

And gone.

* * *

She lays there.

Her eyes are closed and for a long while there is nothing.

She remains in that darkness.

Then she becomes aware of her own breathing and as the ebb and flow of her breath continues her awareness of herself grows.

She can feel her mattress beneath her.

Tentatively, she opens her eyes and almost cries out as she is greeted with complete darkness. She pushes and fights for light and more air, thrashing around and around.

In this way, she eventually frees herself of the duvet in which she had become entrapped.

She lays there breathing heavily with the effort of freeing herself. Relieved to be in her room and bathed in the daylight of the new day.

She is home.

She laughs at the ceiling as she understands that it has all been a dream. A terrible dream made all the more frightening by the way that it seemed so real. But then, how could a dream be real if it featured an overgrown baby using the voices of famous actors?

She laughs some more with the relief of it all. She's back and it has all just been a stupid cheese dream.

Once she is done with laughing, she rolls over to grab her watch and see what time it is, if she were to be honest with herself, she is also going to check the date. The grip of those dreams hasn't loosened itself quite as much as she would like to think and it feels like she has been away for days.

The hour is reasonable and she has the rest of the day ahead of her, a cup of tea beckons from down the stairs. And the day is the very next day, as she expected. And had hoped.

Then, all of a sudden, she drops her watch and it is forgotten.

Her mind gave her some time. It indulged her in fulfilling her intent, and now that she knows the day and that it is seven in the morning, it returns her to the object on her bedside table. The object that was next to the watch as she picked it up.

Her jaw follows the trajectory of her watch and it drops, her lips forming a large O.

Her eyes are wide and her mind refuses to believe the evidence that those eyes are presenting to her. She reaches out a finger and she pokes at the object. Flinching from it as her sense of touch sends messages back to her beleaguered mind – the object is all too real.

Carol sits up with a hyper alertness and looks around the room for other signs. She is not certain what form the signs may take, less still about what they may mean. Finding no further signs, she resorts to a variation of the age old last resort: pinching herself. Only she digs her nails into the palms of her hand so hard and so deep that she draws blood and despite herself she cries.

She cries like she has never cried before, and she cries for a long time. Eventually, through a blur of tears, she returns her gaze to the object on her bedside table. An innocuous object that sits there as though it has always been there, but she knows that cannot be. That nothing like this could be allowed in this room or in this house. Until now.

The object has a simple wooden frame, propped up by a cheap card stand. There is dust on the glass, helping to give the lie that it has always been here. Through the glass is an old photo of a man, a woman and a child.

The child is Carol and she is smiling.

The couple are her mother and her father, Emily and Jacob, and they are also smiling in this snapshot of a family moment.

A family.

Two parents, together and there for their child.

Always and forever.

Carol knows that that photo should always have been there. That it is symbolic. It is reassurance. It is an effort from both those imperfect adults in that photo to do the right thing and to always do the right thing by their child.

The photo is in its rightful place now and Carol suspects that she knows who it is that put this photo here. She wonders where it has been all these years. It is a photo she does not think she has ever seen before and a moment that she cannot recall, but these things do not diminish its importance or the way she feels right now.

The photo is an apology.

The photo is repentance.

It is redemption.

It is a reminder of days past. Happy days.

And it is a promise of the happiness to come.

13

T he end?

The voice of Michael Gambon, or if you prefer, Dumbledore, rose up like a magnificent magical beast and filled the air with an ending.

An ending of sorts.

This ending is not an end. There are no neat endings in life.

Besides, it does not do to pin all of your hopes and expectations on one person, that has a habit of ending in disappointment and sadness, so let's not focus on that one person who has made a few wrong choices in life and who could so easily turn it around with a few better choices.

Life is a series of choices and we can all of us make better choices, if we take the time to think and to care. Kindness is a gift that is available to each and every one of us, but how often do we choose not to bestow it, instead awaiting that self-same kindness from others first. Expecting to receive before we even consider giving.

And yet we all know that we get out of life what we put in.

We also know that life is a miracle and that we are incredibly lucky to be here, in this moment. Not only are we a singular miracle, but we are a part of a greater miracle. Without the miracles that surround us and form a part of our world, we would be nothing. Amount to nothing.

So, is it too much to ask each and every one of us to be at least a little thankful from time to time? To take a moment, take stock and value what it is that we have and in valuing it know that there is no price we can place upon any of it, it is beyond that sort of evaluation and there is a joy to be had in the knowing of this.

All of us get caught up in the detail of a life lived. All of us end up facing the wrong way and looking in the wrong direction. We have to accept that we are flawed creatures and we should forgive ourselves regularly for the nonsensical things that we find ourselves doing, and then we should turn back around and attempt to make a good choice that we know will take us in the right direction.

Because all of us have that option. All of us can make the world a better place, one choice and one step at a time.

Carol has the whole of the rest of her life to consider where the choices she has made have taken her and where they will continue to take her. At any point, she can stop making some of those choices that have done her a disservice and she can start making positive changes in her life.

That she should do this is clear to you and I.

Isn't it more important that we look to ourselves and do that self-same work? I am sure we will discover choices that we can make that will make the world of difference to us and the people around us.

That is an ending, but more importantly, it is a beginning.

You still want to know what happens to Carol, don't you...

* * *

The door.

That door.

She stands at that door again and she takes a deep breath as she yet again faces its challenge.

She is unaware that she is muttering to herself, a soundtrack made by her inner dialogue, the force of will that she is exerting right now spilling out from her. Her body is thrumming with energy, but for once that energy is not anger.

That she is here is enough. She tells herself this and she is almost convinced of it. That is a start in itself.

That it has taken her three previous attempts and almost two weeks to get here appals her and she would be ashamed to admit it to another living soul. She has already resolved to tell three living souls this very thing though. She figures that she owes them that much, but that she owes herself much, much more.

And this is a good start.

The urge to turn and escape the torture of this moment, a constant torture of which she had become unaware as she supressed and normalised it, is strong. But she is stronger. She knows this because it took strength to go through this door when she was a small child. It took strength to be her Dad's champion and wage a silent war on his foes for all of those years.

She cannot falter now.

She must make peace.

Surely waging peace is easier than waging a life-long war?

Who will you be?

The challenge the door makes seems a little different this time, but it is essentially the same as it has always been. Will you betray yourself? Because that is what she has done each and every time she has encountered this door and stepped through it.

"I will be myself," she says quietly to the door that has watched her fail so, so very many times, and she almost bursts into tears for the terrified little girl who was made to do this all alone, time after time.

She holds herself together though, gritting her teeth she raises her fist defiantly to knock at that door.

Only, her hand never reaches the door on this day...

Instead the door, that door, swings open as though the spell has at long last been broken and there before her is her Mum.

Time is an element of this moment and it plays its part, as it so often does, sometimes slowing a moment to an insufferably low pace, or speeding a moment along when it should be savoured. On this occasion, time is an ally. An ally of Carol and an ally of her Mum.

There is no pause between the moment that mother and daughter behold each other across the threshold. Neither of them could explain how they ended up in each other's arms and they will never be asked to, for that would be entirely missing the point.

Carol feels all of the years roll back and she is that child again. The child who stood terrified at that door. Now all of that is gone and all that matters is that she is with her Mum.

And that she is home at last.

About the Author

Jed writes about people. It doesn't matter who or what the people are, nor where they are, it is all about what they do and how they react and behave, when life happens to them.

Jed does his very best not to take himself too seriously. There was a point in his former life where he lost his inner child, having left it in an umbrella rack in the foyer of an office near Liverpool Street Station. He is still doing his best to make amends for that unfortunate oversight and his inner child is not letting it go any time soon.

Jed Cope is the author of seven Ben and Thom books. He has also penned nine further books and a collection of short stories. He is working industriously to add to that number in the mistaken belief that he will be given a day off from writing once he's written his twentieth novel. Unfortunately, his captors got distracted by an ice cream van that had been converted into a travelling pub and completely forgot about Jed. Still, I'm sure it'll all turn out fine in the end. Usually does in circumstances such as these.

The eight books that aren't set in Ben and Thom's universes cover such genres as crime, supernatural and horror. Jed writes as he reads, across a variety of genres. Maybe he likes variety, noting that it is the spice of life, or perhaps he is hedging his bets. Whatever the case may be, he likes to write stories that have a twist or two along the way...

As well as gullible and well-meaning, Jed is a charismatic, enigmatic and pneumatic sort. Having retired from a successful career as a secret multiple F1 Champion, octopus whisperer and technology trillionaire, Jed was abducted from his underground shed where he was working on the next generation of psychic begonias, to do what he does best; make things up.

You can connect with me on:
- https://twitter.com/jed_cope
- https://www.facebook.com/jedcopeauthor

Also by Jed Cope

The Legacy - It's a Right Mess Carol, is Jed Cope's eighteenth book.

If you enjoyed this book, then why not try Do You Remember?

Other books Jed Cope has written...

So far, there are seven Ben and Thom Books:
    The Chair Who Loved Me
    Are Bunnies Electric?
    Smell My Cheese!
    Death and Taxis
    Oh Ben and Thom, Where Art Thou?
    Something Merkin This Way Comes
    Mrs Ben's Boys

Book Eight is a twinkle in the author's eye, but that twinkle is a determined wee beggar and it has a habit of making its way out into the world, so watch this space! The title may even include the word Twinkle...!

There's a children's Ben and Thom Book:
    If Only... The Adventures of an Intergalactic Chair

And eight further books that have nothing whatsoever to do with Ben and Thom:
    The Pipe
    The Entrepreneur's Club

Two for the Show
The Rules of Life
Dear Kids
Do You Remember?
Lola's Path
The Village - A Vampire To Die For
The Legacy - It's a Right Mess Carol

And a collection of short stories:
Locked, Down and Short

Jed intends to add to the list before you've finished reading this one. It's what he does.

Printed in Great Britain
by Amazon

12297270R00081

CPSIA information can be obtained
at www.ICGtesting.com
Printed in the USA
BVHW041659140119
537775BV00007B/660/P

9 780464 704782